NORA EPHRON's
HEARTBURN

HEARTBURN

Nora Ephron

PUBLISHED BY POCKET BOOKS NEW YORK

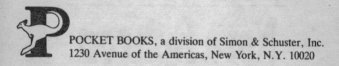

POCKET BOOKS, a division of Simon & Schuster, Inc.
1230 Avenue of the Americas, New York, N.Y. 10020

Copyright © 1983 by Nora Ephron

Published by arrangement with Alfred A. Knopf, Inc.
Library of Congress Catalog Card Number: 82-48999

ISBN: 0-671-49678-6

First Pocket Books printing April, 1984

10 9 8 7 6 5 4 3 2 1

POCKET and colophon are registered trademarks
of Simon & Schuster, Inc.

Printed in the U.S.A.

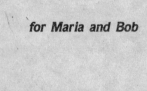

for Maria and Bob

I

The first day I did not think it was funny. I didn't think it was funny the third day either, but I managed to make a little joke about it. "The most unfair thing about this whole business," I said, "is that I can't even date." Well, you had to be there, as they say, because when I put it down on paper it doesn't sound funny. But what made it funny (trust me) is the word "date," which when you say it out loud at the end of a sentence has a wonderful teenage quality, and since I am not a teenager (okay, I'm thirty-eight), and since the reason I was hardly in a position to date on first learning that my second husband had taken a lover was that I was seven months pregnant, I got a laugh on it, though for all I know my group was only laughing because they were trying to cheer me up. I needed cheering up. I was in

7

New York, staying in my father's apartment, I was crying most of the time, and every time I stopped crying I had to look at my father's incredibly depressing walnut furniture and slate-gray lamps, which made me start crying again.

I had gotten on the shuttle to New York a few hours after discovering the affair, which I learned about from a really disgusting inscription to my husband in a book of children's songs she had given him. *Children's* songs. "Now you can sing these songs to Sam" was part of the disgusting inscription, and I can't begin to tell you how it sent me up the wall, the idea of my two-year-old child, my baby, involved in some dopey inscriptive way in this affair between my husband, a fairly short person, and Thelma Rice, a fairly tall person with a neck as long as an arm and a nose as long as a thumb and you should see her legs, never mind her feet, which are sort of splayed.

My father's apartment was empty, my father having been carted off to the loony bin only days before by my sister Eleanor, who is known as the Good Daughter in order to differentiate her from me. My father leads a complicated psychological life along with his third wife, who incidentally happens to be my former best friend Brenda's sister. My father's third wife had been wandering up Third Avenue in a towel the week before, when she was spotted by Renee Fleisher, who went to high school with Brenda and me. Renee Fleisher called my father, who was in no position to help since his crack-up was halfway there, and then she called me in Washington. "I don't believe it," she said. "I just bumped into Brenda's big sister and she says she's married to your father." I myself had found it hard to believe when it happened: to have your father marry your mortal enemy's older sister is a bit too coincidental for my taste, even though I go along with that stuff about small worlds. You have no choice if you're Jewish. "It's fine with me if you marry Brenda's sister," I had said to my father when he called to say he was about to, "but please have her sign a prenuptial agreement so that when you die, none of your fortune ends up with Brenda." So Brenda's big sister signed the agreement, that was three years ago, and now here's Renee Fleisher on the phone to say, hi ho, Brenda's sister married your father and by the way she's wandering up Third Avenue wearing a towel. I turned all this over to my sister Eleanor, who put on her goodness and went over to my father's apartment and got some clothes onto Brenda's sister and sent her to her mother in Miami Beach and took my father to a place called Seven Clouds, which is not an auspicious name for a loony bin, but you'd be amazed how little choice you have about loony bins. Off went my father to dry out and make ashtrays out of leaves, and there sat his apartment in New York, empty.

I had the keys to my father's apartment; I'd stayed there often in the past year because we were broke. When Mark and I got married we were rich and two years later we were broke. Not actually broke—we did have equity. We had a stereo system that had eaten thousands of dollars, and a country house in West Virginia that had eaten tens of thousands of dollars, and a city house in Washington that had eaten hundreds of thousands of dollars, and we had *things*—God, did we have things. We had weather vanes and quilts and carousel horses and stained-glass windows and tin boxes and pocket mirrors and Cadbury chocolate cups and postcards of San Francisco before the earthquake, so we were worth something; we just had no money. It was always a little mystifying to me how we had gone from having so much money to having so little, but now, of course, I understand it all a little better, because the other thing that ate our money was the affair with Thelma Rice. Thelma went to France in the middle of it, and you should see the phone bills.

Not that I knew about the phone bills the day I found the book of children's songs with the disgusting inscription in it. "My darling Mark," it began, "I wanted to give you something to mark what happened today, which makes our future so much clearer. Now you can sing these songs to Sam, and someday we will sing them to him together. I love you. Thelma." That was it. I could hardly believe

it. Well, the truth is I didn't believe it. I looked
at the signature again and tried to make it
come out some other name, a name of someone I didn't know as opposed to someone I did,
but there was the *T* and there was the *a* plain
as day, even if the letters in the middle were a
little squishy, and there's not much you can
do with a name that begins with a *T* and ends
in an *a* but Thelma. Thelma! She had just
been to our house for lunch! She and her
husband Jonathan—actually, they hadn't
come for lunch, they'd stopped by afterward
for dessert, a carrot cake I'd made that had too
much crushed pineapple in it but was still
awfully good compared to Thelma's desserts.
Thelma always makes these gluey puddings.
Thelma, her husband Jonathan (who knew
all about the affair, it turned out), my husband Mark—all three of them sat there while I
waddled around in a drip-dry maternity dress
serving carrot cake to the rest of the guests
and apologizing about the crushed pineapple.

It may seem odd to you that their coming to
lunch bothers me as much as it does, but one
of the worst things about finding out about a
thing like this is that you feel stupid, and the
idea that I actually invited them over and
they actually accepted and all three of them
actually sat there thinking I was some sort of
cheese made it that much worse. The most
mortifying part of it all is that the next day
Thelma called to say thank you and asked for
the carrot cake recipe and I sent it to her. I

removed the crushed pineapple, of course. "Here is the carrot cake recipe," I wrote on a postcard, "with the kinks out of it." I'm afraid I put a little face with a smile next to the recipe. I am not the sort of person who puts little faces on things, but there are times when nothing else will do. Right now, for instance, I would like to put a little face at the very end of this sentence, only this one would have a frown on it.

I should point out that although I could hardly believe Mark was having an affair with Thelma, I knew he was having an affair with someone. That was how I came upon the songbook in the first place: I was poking around in his drawers, looking for clues. But Thelma! It made me really angry. It would have been one thing if he'd gotten involved with a little popsy, but he'd gone off and had an affair with a person who was not only a giant but a clever giant. I cannot tell you how many parties we'd come home from while this affair was being secretly conducted and I'd said, while taking off my clothes, "God, Thelma said such an amusing thing tonight." Then I would repeat it, word for word, to Mark. Talk about being a fool! *Talk about being a fool!* I even knew Thelma was having an affair! Everyone did. She had taken to talking indiscriminately and openly about the possibility that her husband Jonathan would be dispatched to some faraway State Department post and she would stay behind in Washington and buy a condominium.

"She's talking about condominiums," my friend Betty Searle called up to say one day. "Obviously she's involved with someone."

"Are you sure?" I said.

"Of course I'm sure," said Betty. "The question is who." She thought for a minute. "Maybe it's Senator Campbell," she said. "He's talking about condominiums, too."

"Senators always talk about condominiums," I said.

"That's true," said Betty, "but who else could it be?"

"I'll ask Mark," I said.

"Do you think Thelma Rice is having an affair with Senator Campbell?" I said to Mark that night.

"No," he said.

"Well, she's having an affair with someone," I said.

"How do you know?" he said.

"She's talking about buying a condominium if Jonathan is sent to Bangladesh," I said.

"Jonathan's not going to be sent to Bangladesh," said Mark.

"Why not?" I said.

"Because we still care about Bangladesh," said Mark.

"Then Upper Volta," I said.

Mark shook his head, as if he couldn't believe he'd been dragged into such a hopelessly girlish conversation, and went back to reading *House & Garden*. Shortly after that, the talk of condominiums stopped.

"Thelma's not talking about condominiums anymore," Betty called up to say one day. "What do you think it means?"

"Maybe it's over," I said.

"No," said Betty. "It's not over."

"How do you know?" I said.

"She had her legs waxed," said Betty, and then, very slowly, added, "for the first time." And then, even more slowly: "And it's not even summer yet."

"I see what you mean," I said.

Betty Searle really was a witch about these things—about many things, in fact. She could go to a dinner party in Washington and the next day she could tell you who was about to be fired—just on the basis of the seating plan! She should have been a Kremlinologist in the days when everything we knew about Russia was based on the May Day photograph. Twitches, winks and shrugs that seemed like mere nervous mannerisms to ordinary mortals were gale force indicators to Betty. Once, for example, at a cocktail reception, she realized that the Secretary of Health, Education and Welfare was about to be canned because the Vice-President's wife kissed him hello and then patted him on the shoulder.

"Anyone pats you on the shoulder when you're in the cabinet, you're in big trouble," Betty said the next day.

"But it was only the Vice-President's wife," I said.

Betty shook her head, as if I would never ever learn. Later that day, she called the Secretary of Health, Education and Welfare and told him that his days were numbered, but he was so busy fighting with the tobacco lobby that he paid no attention. Two days later, the tobacco lobby rented the grand ballroom of the Washington Hilton to celebrate his ouster, and the Secretary of Health, Education and Welfare started preparing to go on the lecture circuit.

"So who do you think Thelma's involved with?" Betty said.

"It could be anyone," I said.

"Of course it could be anyone," said Betty, "but who is it?"

"What about Congressman Toffler?" I said.

"You think so?" said Betty.

"She's always talking about how brilliant he is," I said.

"And she seated him next to herself at her last dinner party," said Betty.

"I'll ask Mark," I said. "He was seated on her other side."

"Do you think Thelma Rice is having an affair with Congressman Toffler?" I asked Mark that night.

"No," said Mark.

"Well, whoever she's having an affair with, she's still having it," I said.

"How do you know?" said Mark.

"She had her legs waxed," I said. "And it's only May."

"The Ladies' Central is busy this week, isn't it?" said Mark. "Who'd you hear that from?"

"Betty," I said.

Mark went back to reading *Architectural Digest*, and shortly thereafter Thelma Rice went to France for a few weeks, and Betty and I moved on to the subject of the President's assistant, who was calling Betty in the middle of the night and saying, "Meet me in the Rotunda and I'll tickle your tits," and other bizarre remarks encompassing Washington and sex.

"What should I do about it?" Betty said one day at lunch.

"Tell him if he does it again you'll call the newspapers," I said.

"I did," said Betty, "and you know what he said? He said, 'You haven't lived till you've squeezed my Washington Post.' Then he cackled madly." She poked at her Chicken Salad Albert Gore. "Anyway, I can't prove it's him," she said, "although Thelma always says he's a notorious letch."

"That's what Mark always says, too," I said.

I should have figured it out, of course. By the time I did, the thing had been going on for months, for seven months—for exactly as long as my pregnancy. I should have known, should have suspected something sooner, especially since Mark spent so much time that summer at the dentist. There sat Sam and I in

West Virginia, making air holes in jars full of caterpillars, and there went Mark, in and out of Washington, to have root canals and gum treatments and instructions in flossing and an actual bridge, never once complaining about the inconvenience or the pain or the boredom of having to listen to Irwin Tannenbaum, D.D.S., drone on about his clarinet. Then it was fall, and we were all back in Washington, and every afternoon, Mark would emerge from his office over the garage and say he was going out to buy socks, and every evening he would come home empty-handed and say, you would not believe how hard it is to find a decent pair of socks in this city. Four weeks it took me to catch on! Inexcusable, especially since it was exactly the sort of thing my first husband said when he came home after spending the afternoon in bed with my best friend Brenda, who subsequently and as a result became my mortal enemy. "Where were you the last six hours?" I said to my first husband. "Out buying light bulbs," he said. Light bulbs. Socks. What am I doing married to men who come up with excuses like this? Once, when I was married to my first husband, I went off to meet a man in a hotel room at six in the morning and told my husband I was going out to be on the *Today* show; it never even crossed his mind to turn on the television set to watch. Now, that's what I call a decent job of lying! Not that it does any good to prove my ingenuity; it doesn't matter how smart you are if both your husbands manage to prove how dumb you are as easily as mine had.

Of course, my fling with the man in the hotel room happened a long time ago—before my divorce, before I met Mark, before I decided to marry him and become an incorrigible believer in fidelity. It is of course hideously ironic that the occasion for my total conversion to fidelity was my marriage to Mark, but timing has never been my strong point; and in any case, the alternative, infidelity, doesn't work. You have only a certain amount of energy, and when you spread it around, everything gets confused, and the first thing you know, you can't remember which one you've told which story to, and the next thing you know, you're moaning, "Oh, Morty, Morty, Morty," when what you mean is "Oh, Sidney, Sidney, Sidney," and the next thing you know, you think you're in love with both of them simply because you've been raised to believe that the only polite response to the words "I love you" is "I love you too," and the next thing you know, you think you're in love with only one of them, because you're too guilty to handle loving them both.

After I found the book with the disgusting inscription in it, I called Mark. I'm embarrassed to tell you where I called him—okay, I'll tell you: I called him at his shrink's. He goes to a Guatemalan shrink over in Alexandria who looks like Carmen Miranda and has a dog named Pepito. "Come home immediately," I said. "I know about you and Thelma Rice." Mark did not come home immediately. He came home two hours later because—are you ready for this?—THELMA RICE WAS ALSO AT THE SHRINK'S. They were having a double session! At the family rate!! I did not know this at the time. Not only did Thelma Rice and Mark see Dr. Valdez and her Chihuahua, Pepito, once a week, but so did Thelma's husband, Jonathan Rice, the undersecretary of state for Middle Eastern affairs. Mark and Thelma saw Chiquita Banana together, and Jonathan Rice saw her alone—and that man has something to do with making peace in the Middle East!

When Mark finally came home, I was completely prepared. I had rehearsed a speech about how I loved him and he loved me and we had to work at our marriage and we had a baby and we were about to have another— really the perfect speech for the situation except that I had misapprehended the situation. "I am in love with Thelma Rice," he said when he arrived home. That was the situation. He then told me that although he was in love with Thelma Rice, they were not having an affair. (Apparently he thought I could handle the fact that he was in love with her but not the fact that he was having sex with her.) "That is a lie," I said to him, "but if it's true"—you see, there was a part of me that wanted to think it was true even though I knew it wasn't: the man is capable of having sex with a venetian blind—"if it's true, you might as well be having an affair with her, because it's free." Some time later, after going on saying all these lovey-dovey things about Thelma, and after saying he wouldn't give her up, and after saying that I was a shrew and a bitch and a nag and a kvetch and a grouse and that I hated Washington (the last charge was undeniably true), he said that he nonetheless expected me to stay with him. At that moment, it crossed my mind that he might be crazy. I sat there on the couch with tears rolling down my face and my fat belly resting on my thighs, I screwed up my courage, and when Mark finished his sixteenth speech about how wonderful Thelma Rice was compared to me, I said to him, "You're crazy." It took every ounce of self-confidence I had.

"You're wrong," he said.

He's right, I thought. I'm wrong.

Well, we went around in circles. And then he asked me if I wanted to be alone for a while. I guess he wanted to drive over to Thelma's to tell her he had held fast to their love. It didn't matter. He drove off and I scooped up Sam and a suitcase full of Pampers, called a taxi, and left for the airport.

II

*O*ne thing I have never understood is how to work it so that when you're married, things keep happening to you. Things happen to you when you're single. You meet new men, you travel alone, you learn new tricks, you read Trollope, you try sushi, you buy nightgowns, you shave your legs. Then you get married, and the hair grows in. I love the everydayness of marriage, I love figuring out what's for dinner and where to hang the pictures and do we owe the Richardsons, but life does tend to slow to a crawl. The whole summer Mark was secretly seeing Thelma Rice while pretending to be at the dentist, I was cooking. That's what I do for a living—I write cookbooks. And while I did discover a fairly revolutionary and absolutely foolproof way to make a four-minute egg, and had gotten to the point where

I simply could not make a bad vinaigrette, this was not exactly the stuff of drama. (Even now, I cannot believe Mark would want to risk losing that vinaigrette. You just don't bump into vinaigrettes that good.) Before that, there had been a lot of time spent on swatches and couches and floor plans. It was almost as if Mark had a career as a columnist and I had a career as a food person and our marriage had a career as a fighter with contractors. First we fought with the Washington contractor, who among other atrocities managed to install our carpet on the sixth floor of a Washington department store; then we fought with the West Virginia contractor, who forgot the front door. "No one uses front doors in the country anyway," he said when we pointed it out, which was also what he said about the paper-towel rack and the medicine cabinet. Then we hired Laszlo Pump, a Hungarian trouble-shooter, to clean up the mess the other two contractors had made, and that was when the real trouble began. Laszlo ripped out the living room wall and vanished. We called him at home and got his wife. She said his father had died. A week later she said his dog had died. A week later she said his analyst had died. Finally we reached Laszlo. He said he had cancer.

"He has cancer," I said when I hung up the phone.

"Bullshit," said Mark.

"People don't lie about that," I said.

"Yes they do," said Mark. "Contractors do. They lie about everything. Look, we'll go to his house. We'll see how he looks. If he looks okay I'll kill him."

"We can't go to his house," I said.

"Why not?" said Mark.

"Because we don't know where he lives."

"We'll look it up," said Mark.

"We can't look it up," I said. "He has an unlisted address."

"What are you talking about?" said Mark.

"It's the latest thing," I said.

"What kind of person has an unlisted address?" Mark said. "I'll tell you what kind. The kind that doesn't want to be dead. The kind that people are trying to kill all the time."

"Why are you angry at me?" I said.

"I'm not angry at you," said Mark.

"Then why are you shouting at me?" I said.

"Because you're the only one who's here," said Mark.

I burst into tears. "I hate it when you get angry," I said.

"I'm not angry at you," said Mark. "I love you. I'm not angry at you."

"I know," I said, "but it scares me. It reminds me of my father."

"I'm not your father," said Mark. "Repeat after me, 'Mark Feldman is not my father.'"

"Mark Feldman is not my father," I said.

"Am I fat?" said Mark.

"No," I said.

"Am I bald?"

"No."

"Do I smell of Dr. Scholl's foot pads?"

"No," I said.

"I rest my case," said Mark.

It always ended up like that in the end—us against the world, Washington's bravest couple in combat with the entire service industry and their answering machines—but the point I want to make is this: I sat on that plane to New York in a state of total misery, yet part of me was secretly relieved to be done with swatches and couches and fights with contractors, and that part of me was thinking: Okay, Rachel Samstat, finally something is happening to you.

That's my name—Rachel Samstat. It's always been Rachel Samstat. I held on to it through both my marriages—through the first because I never liked my first husband's last name enough to change mine to it, and through the second because I was by then known in a small and modest way as Rachel Samstat. The cookbooks I write do well. They're very personal and chatty—they're cookbooks in an almost incidental way. I write chapters about friends or relatives or trips or experiences, and work in the recipes peripherally. Then, of course, the television show came along, which made the books sell even better.

How I got my own show is probably something you're wondering. I'm not exactly a conventional television personality, although I suppose I'm somewhat conventional when it comes to public television, which is what my show was on, not network. "Too New York" is what the last network that was approached about me responded, which is a cute way of being anti-Semitic, but who cares? I'd rather be too New York than too anything else. Anyway, I don't belong on a network. I have the kind of odd and interesting features that work out all right in life but not at all on the screen, so I'm far better off on public television, where the producers and cameramen are used to Julia Child and are pathetically grateful that I'm not quite as tall. Also, there's my blink. I blink. "Hi, I'm Rachel Samstat"— saying that, looking directly at the camera, I blink fifty or sixty times minimum. It's the looking at the camera that makes me do it; when I'm looking at a person, or a pork roast, my blinks go down to near normal.

After we taped the first show and discovered the blink, Richard, my producer, suggested I go see a professional television coach, who specialized in voices but was willing to undertake a little eyelid work on the side. She kept telling me she'd never had a failure, probably to encourage me, but the effect was to make me absolutely determined to be her first, which I was.

"I don't think I can fix the blink," she told Richard after several sessions, "but I can probably do a little something with the voice."

"We like the voice," said Richard, and thank God, because there wasn't much left of me by then that someone hadn't taken a swipe at, usually using the definite article. The voice. The blink. The hair. The chin. "She has a quality onscreen not unlike Howard Cosell," someone high up at the station is supposed to have said, and even though I choose to think he meant it as a compliment—he meant I'm the sort of person you feel strongly about one way or another—Howard Cosell was not exactly what I had in mind. What I had in mind was Imogene Coca or Elaine May. Anyway, the important thing is that I do happen to have a funny voice, and it makes people laugh. It works on television, although there's no way a voice coach would understand that, since her job is to teach everyone to sound like David Brinkley.

It's really because of Richard that the television show came up at all. I was on a talk show promoting *My Grandmother's Cookies* when Richard saw me. Actually, it was Phil Donahue he saw me on. Richard is hooked on Phil Donahue. He says that if Sigmund Freud had watched Phil Donahue he would never have wondered what women want. There I was, fielding questions about piecrust and doing my Jewish prince routine, when Richard got the idea it might make a series—me and my relatives and my friends and a few famous strangers, talking about food, talking about the role food plays in life, doing a little cooking, a middlebrow Julia Child crossed with a highbrow Dinah Shore. How we got away with it I don't know, except that we threw Proust and his madeleines into the opening credits, and I managed to get Isaac Bashevis Singer to make noodle kugel on the pilot. Also, the show cost next to nothing to produce, and what little it cost was underwritten by an oil company where someone I used to date is now in charge of parceling out money to public television. I dated him when he was Jewish—now that he works at the oil company you can't exactly tell. He was so Jewish when I dated him that he taught Hebrew school, and I, who at that point had had no Jewish education whatsoever, learned about Purim and good Queen Esther and the wicked Haman from him one night in a dormitory at Harvard while he stuck one and then two and then three fingers into me. This was before the discovery of the clitoris, when there was far too much sticking of fingers into things and not nearly enough playing around with the outsides; still, it was a nice enough introduction to the origins of Hamantaschen pastries, and I retain a special and absurd affection for Purim in spite of the fact that I have always hated Hamantaschen. That isn't true. Mark's Aunt Florence makes good Hamantaschen. Aunt Florence, who raised Mark, is a great cook; her triumph, which she serves on Thanksgiving along with the turkey, is a brisket cooked with sauerkraut and brown sugar, and it sounds perfectly awful, I know, but it's truly one of the most delicious things I've ever eaten.

I'd been planning to have Mark's Aunt Florence on the next thirteen-week cycle of my television show to discuss the brisket, as well as her tzimmes and gefilte fish, but I don't really see how I'm going to be able to now that all this has come about. I don't like blaming family members for what goes wrong with children, because someday when my kids are arrested for grand larceny I don't want anyone looking accusingly at me, but Mark's behavior was so obviously Florence's fault that even Florence knew it. "It must be my fault" were in fact her first words on the subject when I called to tell her I had gone to New York because her nephew had fallen in love with Thelma Rice. "Don't be silly," I said in reply, but what I was thinking was: You bet your sweet ass it is. Jewish princes are made, not born.

RACHEL SAMSTAT'S JEWISH PRINCE ROUTINE

You know what a Jewish prince is, don't you?
    (Cocks her eyebrow)
If you don't, there's an easy way to recognize one. A simple sentence. "Where's the butter?"

*(A long pause here, because the laugh
starts slowly and builds)*

Okay. We all know where the butter is, don't
we?

(A little smile)

The butter is in the refrigerator.

(Beat)

The butter is in the refrigerator in the little
compartment in the door marked "Butter."

(Beat)

But the Jewish prince doesn't mean "Where's
the butter?" He means "Get me the butter."
He's too clever to say "Get me" so he says
"Where's."

(Beat)

And if you say to him—

(Shouting)

"in the refrigerator"—

(Resume normal voice)

and he goes to look, an interesting thing happens, a medical phenomenon that has not
been sufficiently remarked upon.

(Beat)

The effect of the refrigerator light on the male
cornea.

(Beat)

Blindness.

(A long beat)

"I don't see it anywhere."

(Pause)

"Where's the butter" is only one of the ways
the Jewish prince reveals himself. Sometimes

he puts it a different way. He says, "Is there any butter?"

(*Beat*)

We all know whose fault it is if there isn't, don't we.

(*Beat*)

When he's being really ingenious, he puts it in a way that's meant to sound as if what he needs most of all from you is your incredible wisdom and judgment and creativity. He says, "How do you think butter would taste with this?"

(*Beat*)

He's usually referring to dry toast.

(*Beat*)

I've always believed that the concept of the Jewish princess was invented by a Jewish prince who couldn't get his wife to fetch him the butter.

I was not raised as a Jewish princess. Sometimes I'm accused of being one because I'm not exactly the outdoor type, but I grew up a scrappy little athlete with a scrappy little mother who wanted me to have a flashy career like her own. I wonder what she would have made of my work. My mother was a good recreational cook, but what she basically believed about cooking was that if you worked hard and prospered, someone else would do it for you.

My mother was an agent in Hollywood, a

lady agent, a classic forties career woman: she had short hair and bangs, she wore suits with shoulder pads, and she talked in a gravelly voice. She handled what were known in the business as specialty acts, which is to say mostly midgets. After they stopped making movies like *The Wizard of Oz*, the midget market dried up and she moved into actors with scars. In the meantime, we had a lot of midgets hanging around the house, and as a result my mother often served food that was a little too bite-sized. My sister Eleanor gets very churlish about my mother's cooking, and she always points out that my mother's fling with rumaki lasted considerably longer than it should have; but Eleanor hates to give credit where credit is due, and the fact is that my mother had enormous flair when she was paying attention, and when she didn't feel like paying attention she threw in a lot of butter. She could also Keep Help, which I was raised to believe was no small thing; indeed, I was raised to believe that almost the worst thing that could be said about you after you grew up was that you couldn't.

Every New Year's Day, my parents had a big party, and their friends came over and bet on the Rose Bowl and argued about which of the players on either team were Jewish, and my mother served her famous lox and onions and eggs, which took her the entire first half to make. It took her so long, in fact, that I really don't have time to give you the recipe, because it takes up a lot of space to explain how slowly and painstakingly she did everything, sautéing the onions over a tiny flame so none of them would burn, throwing more and more butter into the pan, cooking the eggs so slowly that my father was always sure they wouldn't be ready until the game was completely over and everyone had gone home. We should have known my mother was crazy years before we did just because of the maniacal passion she brought to her lox and onions and eggs, but we didn't. Another thing my mother was famous for serving was a big ham along with her casserole of lima beans and pears. A couple of years ago, I was in Los Angeles promoting *Uncle Seymour's Beef Borscht* and a woman said to me at a party, "Wasn't your mother Bebe Samstat?" and when I said yes, she said, "I have her recipe for lima beans and pears." I like to think it would have amused my mother to know that there is someone in Hollywood who remembers her only for her lima beans and pears, but it probably wouldn't have. Anyway, here's how you make it: Take 6 cups defrosted lima beans, 6 pears peeled and cut into slices, ½ cup molasses, ½ cup chicken stock, ½ onion chopped, put into a heavy casserole, cover and bake 12 hours at 200°. That's the sort of food she loved to serve, something that looked like plain old baked beans and then turned out to have pears up its sleeve. She also made a bouillabaisse with Swiss chard in it. Later on, she got too serious about food—started making egg rolls from scratch, things like that—and one night she resigned from the kitchen permanently over a lobster Cantonese that didn't work out, and that was the beginning of the end.

Shortly after that, she went into her blue-chip stamp phase. She wasn't alone, of course. It was 1963, and there were a lot of American women who were saving blue-chip stamps and green stamps and plaid stamps and whatever stamps their supermarkets were giving out; still, ladies in suits with shoulder pads were supposed to have more sense. My mother, who had spent years avoiding supermarkets, made at least one trip a day to the local Thriftimart. (The scar-face market had gone pretty dry on her at this point, and she had very little else to do.) She would get into her 1947 Studebaker and set off for a day in the aisles. She developed passionate and brief attachments to new products. One month she fell in love with instant minced onions. Another month it was Pepperidge Farm raspberry turnovers. The next it was frozen chopped chives. She would return home with her bags of groceries, leave them in the kitchen for the housekeeper to empty, and go up to her bedroom, where the card table was equipped with one of those little sponge-and-jar contraptions you use when you have a lot of stamps to stick.

I was living in New York at the time, and I

heard about most of this from my sister
Eleanor, who was perfecting her sanctimoni-
ousness under the aegis of my mother's pro-
gressive insanity, but I saw a little of it first-
hand when my mother arrived in Manhattan
one day with a ten-speed blender she had
purchased for me with twenty-six books of
blue-chip stamps. She had carried it onto the
plane and held it on her lap all the way to New
York. The next day my apartment was bur-
glarized, and they took the blender, complete
with warranty. They also took my typewriter,
the television set, and my gold bracelet. My
mother surveyed the wreckage and then, instead of just going out to buy a new blender for
sixteen dollars, went off to the nearby A & P
and spent six hundred dollars on groceries,
just for the plaid stamps. Then she returned
to my apartment and began pasting them into
stamp books. That's what she was doing when
the police finally arrived—sitting there at the
table, laughing her gravelly laugh and licking
every so often as the two policemen told us
what they thought were a lot of rollicking
stories about New Yorkers who'd been bur-
glarized of all the presents under their Christmas trees. We all had a drink, and then we all
had another, and four hours later my mother
was singing "When that midnight choochoo
leaves for Alabam'" and the policeman whose
lap she was sitting on was taking little nips at
her shoulder. Then she got up and did a tap
dance to "Puttin' On the Ritz" and passed out

in the middle of it. It was a fabulous pass-out as those things go. She was in midair when it happened—she had both her legs up to one side, and she'd just managed to click her heels together when her eyes clanged shut and she slid on one side of her leg to the floor. I put her to bed.

"Was I very bad?" she said on the way to the airport the next day.

"Not really," I said.

"Please say I was," she said.

My father was a specialty act himself, though not in any formal sense. He was a character actor—he worked under the name of Harry Stratton, the name he still uses—but he played the kind of characters who have no character: he played kindly lawyers and kindly doctors and kindly teachers, and he said kindly things to whatever leading actor was about to lose heart in his fight to discover penicillin or defeat the outlaws or rout the Nazis. He made a lot of money—so did my mother—and they invested it in Tampax stock, and one day they were rich, and a good thing they were, because my mother's medical bills were enormous. She drank and drank and drank and finally one day her stomach swelled up like a Cranshaw melon and they took her to a very fashionable hospital for rich people with cirrhosis and the doctors clucked and said there was nothing that could be done. My parents had moved to New York by this time, and my mother's hospital room had a

view of the East River. She lay there slowly
dying, with my father impatiently standing
by. "Pull the plug," he would say to the doctors, and the doctors would calmly explain
that there was no plug, there was just the
wasting away of life. A few of her former
clients came to see her—the scar faces fright-
ened the nurses and the midgets made whoop-
ee on the electric wheelchairs—and now and
then she came into focus and made deals. "I
think we can get you a hundred thou on the
next one," she would say; she hadn't handled
a client in years, but she went rattling on
about points and box office and below the line
and above the line. The nurse would bring
lunch. "I think I'll take it in the commissary,"
she'd say. One day my father called and said,
"You'd better come. I think this is it." Of
course, he telephoned every day and said that,
but it always sounded like wishful thinking;
now, finally, I knew he must be right. I went
straight to the hospital, and when I went into
her room she was sleeping. Suddenly she
opened her eyes and looked at me. "I just
screwed Darryl Zanuck on the remake," she
said, and gave a little croak, which I didn't
know at the moment was a significant thing,
the actual croak—I thought it was just her
gravelly laugh—and died.

"Mother's gone," said the nurse. Not "Your
mother" but "Mother." I stared at the nurse,
stunned not so much by my mother's death,
which after all had been promised for months

and, as far as my father was concerned, was long overdue, but by the nurse's presumption. "You can call your mother Mother," I snapped, "but you can't call my mother Mother." The nurse gave me one of those withering looks that are meant to make you feel as if your thoroughly understandable rage is mere female hysteria. She pulled the sheet over my mother's face. "We're going to take Mother away now," she said in a tone so condescending that I became even more wild with anger. "She's not your mother," I shouted. "On top of which, she's not gone, she's dead. Do you hear me? *Dead*. And what you're going to take away is her body, so call it a body. Call it a corpse, for Christ's sake." The nurse was now looking at me with an expression of complete horror, which I thought at the time was on account of my behavior, but it wasn't really; it was complete horror at what was happening behind me, which was that my mother had chosen that moment to make a full recovery. The sheet began rising like a slow-motion poltergeist, and then, in a burst, my mother whipped off the cloth and shouted: "Ta da!" Then she fainted. "Fainted dead away" is what the nurse said, which just goes to show you another anomaly of hospital life, which is that they only use the word "dead" when it doesn't apply.

"We thought you were dead," I said a few minutes later, when my mother came to.

"I was," she said, "I was." She shook her

head slightly, as if trying to remember a fuzzy dream. "I floated away in a white organdy dress and black patent-leather Mary Janes," she said. "I looked like Baby Snooks. I tried to get something to wear that was more dignified, but the dignified clothes were being used on another set." She nodded; it was all coming back now. "I looked down, and there was your father, clicking a clapboard that read: 'Bebe's Death, Take One.' The camera started rolling. I was floating further and further away. I was definitely dead. Your father sold the Tampax stock and bought himself a Borsalino hat. 'Print,' he said. 'It's a wrap.'" She began tapping her breastbone defiantly. "*I* was the one who sat next to Bernard Baruch at a dinner party in 1944 and heard him say, 'Buy something people use once and throw away.' *I* was the one who stuck a Tampax into my twat in 1948 and came out of the bathroom and said, 'See if this is traded over the counter.' *I* was the one who made us rich, and now the bastard is going off and spending my money on bimbos while I'm stuck in goyishe heaven in an inappropriate costume. Fuck this, I said to myself, and at that moment I came back."

The next day, when I went to see her, she was sitting up in bed smoking Kools and doing the Double-Crostic. "I have experienced a miracle," she said. "You know what that means, don't you?"

"No," I said.

"It means there's a God," she said. "If you

believe in miracles you have to believe in God. One follows from the other."

"No it doesn't," I said. "It doesn't follow at all. It doesn't have to be the sort of miracle someone's in charge of. It could just have been an accident of some sort. Or a dream. Or a misdiagnosis on the part of the nurse."

My mother shook her head. "I was dead," she said. "You should have seen it up there. Fluffy white clouds, and little angels with pink cheeks playing tiny harps."

"Lyres," I said.

"Miss Smart and her college education," said my mother.

A week later, she checked out of the hospital, filed for divorce, and went to New Mexico to find God. And she did. She found God and she married him. His name was Mel, he honestly believed he was God, and as my first husband Charlie said at the time, "If there's one thing we know about God, it's that he's not named Mel." Mel took my mother for every penny she had, plus Charlie's old Swedish-modern couch and a set of flatware I was very attached to. Then she died again, this time for good.

I would like to ask her what a person who is seven months pregnant is supposed to do when her husband turns out to be in love with someone else, but the truth is she probably wouldn't have been much help. Even in the old days, my mother was a washout at hard-core mothering; what she was good at were clever remarks that made you feel immensely sophisticated and adult and, if you thought about it at all, foolish for having wanted anything so mundane as some actual nurturing. Had I been able to talk to her at this moment of crisis, she would probably have said something fabulously brittle like "Take notes." Then she would have gone into the kitchen and toasted almonds. You melt some butter in a frying pan, add whole blanched almonds, and sauté until they're golden brown with a few little burned parts. Drain lightly and salt and eat with a nice stiff drink. "Men are little boys," she would have said as she lifted her glass. "Don't stir or you'll bruise the ice cubes."

III

Maybe you think I walked out on Mark awfully fast if I was really so in love with him, but I probably wouldn't have if it wasn't for my therapist. I left that part out, and I hate to bring it up because until now you've been thinking that Mark was the one with the unconventional shrink, and now you're going to see we both were. Oh, well. I have a therapist named Vera Maxwell. She's fifty-eight years old and quite beautiful, she has creamy white skin and curly black hair and she wears bright red lipstick and caftans. She's famous, really, she goes on talk shows and has a lot of celebrity patients, and every so often she has to fly off to co-host Merv Griffin, or she has to take a phone call in the middle of a session from someone having a crisis at the Cannes Film Festival.

Vera is a wonderful therapist. She is loving, caring, giving and unrelenting. Of course, when I first went to her, I was unhappily married to Charlie, and now nine years had passed and I was unhappily married to Mark, and that might not sound like progress. But trust me. You'll have to trust me, because there's no real way to convey what she does in her office that doesn't sound like some sort of Yiddish mumbo jumbo. She tells the kreplach joke a lot, and the one about the man from Minsk meeting the man from Pinsk. I will tell you the kreplach joke, but the truth is you need an accent to tell it well; I would throw in a recipe for kreplach as well, but it's a pain in the ass to make kreplach.

THE KREPLACH JOKE

Once upon a time there was a little boy who hated kreplach. Every time he saw a piece of kreplach in the soup he screamed, "Aaaaah, kreplach!" So his mother decided to teach him not to be afraid of kreplach. She took him into the kitchen and rolled out some dough. "Just like a pancake," she said. "Just like a pancake," said the little boy. Then she took a piece of meat and rolled it into a ball. "Just like a meatball," she said. "Just like a meatball," said the little boy. Then she rolled up the meat in the dough and held it up. "Just like a dumpling," she said. "Just like a dumpling," said the little boy. Then she dropped it into the soup and put it in front of the little boy, and he screamed, "Aaaaah, kreplach!"

Anyway, the thing about Vera is that she's very direct; she's not one of those shrinks who sit there impassively and say "Mmmmhmmm" every so often. After Mark told me he was in love with Thelma Rice and left me to be alone for a while, I called up Vera in New York and told her what had happened, and do you know what she said? She said, "He's disgusting." That threw me a little, because even though I knew that Vera was no slouch at calling a spade a spade, it seemed awfully strong.

"What should I do?" I said.

"What should you do?" Vera replied.

That may not look like a direct response, but it was. She said, "What should you do?" with her voice rising on the word "do," and it was as if there was only one possible thing to do and how could I possibly wonder what it was. But I hung in there; I tried to get her to be a little more specific.

"Yes, what should I do?" I said.

"Is this what you want?" Vera said. "Is this what you want in a husband?"

Well, of course it wasn't what I wanted in a husband. On the other hand, what I wanted in a husband was Mark. At least that's what I'd thought I wanted. Could I help it if Mark didn't measure up to Vera's ideas of a husband? Vera has a husband to match her ideas —his name is Niccolo, and he has a white beard and he wears crisp seersucker suits and straw hats that he tips, and Vera says that the sex she has with Niccolo is as good after twenty years of marriage as it was in the beginning, which is almost the most depressing thing she says since no one else can say that except Vera, but if Vera says it there must be something to it; and what's more, what's worse in a way, is that Vera says she is never bored by Niccolo and he is never bored by her because they never tell the same stories twice. She told me this one day when I was still married to Charlie.

"Never?" I said.

"Never," said Vera, but if she ever did tell a story twice, she said, she would change it around a little so that Niccolo would still find it interesting. Myself, I never change a story. I never even change an *inflection* in a story once it's working. Mark, on the other hand, changes his stories every time he tells them, by making them longer. He has a story he tells about his first day of work in the newspaper business. He went to his office his first day in the newspaper business in a brand-new white suit, and they told him he had to wash the carbon paper, and he believed them, and he went into the men's room and turned on the water and the carbon splattered all over his brand-new white suit. It's a good story. Mark told it to me the night we met. We all have stories like that, stories we rely on to establish our charm in the beginning of relationships. I tell one about wanting to play the ukulele in the school orchestra. They asked me what instrument I wanted to play, and I said the ukulele, and they said, but there's no ukulele in the school orchestra, and I said, then what can I play that's like the ukulele, and they said the viola. That story doesn't sound so charming on the page, but I tell it very well. In any case, by the time Mark fell in love with Thelma Rice, the story about his first day in the newspaper business had turned into a novella.

"Well, is it?" said Vera. "Is this what you want in a husband?"

"I guess not," I said weakly, and left for the plane.

I worry about telling you this kind of story. Psychoanalysis has done strange things to my dialogue, and when I talk about it I sound a little like one of those starlets on *The Tonight Show* who's just stumbled onto Eastern philosophy or feminism or encounter therapy or any other system of thought that explains everything in the universe in eight minutes. Pick a dream, any dream—I'll analyze it and give you a pep talk. This used to cause a lot of friction between me and Mark. When I first met him, he had a recurrent nightmare that Henry Kissinger was chasing him with a knife, and I said it was really his father and he said it was really Henry Kissinger, and I said it was really his father and he said it was really Henry Kissinger, and this went on for months until he started going to the Central American shrinkette, who said Henry Kissinger was really his younger sister. That's almost the only good thing I can say about Our Lady of the Castanets: Mark's going to her at least ended our conflict over psychoanalysis. In fact, he was converted overnight. "What's really bothering you?" he would say. Or: "What does that remind you of?" Or: "That sounds hostile to me." Or: "I'm not your mother." All this happened before we got married, and I found it incredibly seductive.

So we got married and I got pregnant and I gave up my New York apartment and moved to Washington. Talk about mistakes. There I was, a regular at the Thalia, a connoisseur of the latest goat cheeses, an expert on alternate routes to Long Island—there I was, trying to hold up my end in a city where you can't even buy a decent bagel. I don't mean to make it sound as if it's all about being Jewish, but that's another thing about Washington. It makes you feel really Jewish if that's what you are. It's not just that there are so many Gentiles there; it's that the Gentiles are so Gentile. Listen, even the Jews there are sort of Gentile. Not that I complained. I can work anywhere, I said bravely. I had a new husband, and then I had a new baby, and then I had another baby coming, and meanwhile I had my friends and a kitchen stove with six burners. *Uncle Seymour's Beef Borscht* made the best-seller list and two weeks later I was in the Sunday *Times* crossword puzzle, 26 across—Uncle Seymour's niece, it said.

Every so often I would fly to New York for one thing or another, and would go by to see Vera. I had really graduated from therapy by then, but I liked to stop in for an oil check from time to time. I would tell her I was okay, really I was, I was working hard, things were good with me and Mark, the baby was wonderful, and then, after the session, I would walk into Balducci's and there would be the arugola and radicchio and fresh basil and sorrel and sugar snap peas and six kinds of sprouts, and I would think to myself: Even the vegetables in New York are better.

It's not just the vegetables, of course. I look out the window and I see the lights and the skyline and the people on the street rushing around looking for action, love, and the world's greatest chocolate chip cookie, and my heart does a little dance. The little dance my heart was doing as I looked out the window of my father's apartment was not exactly a polka, but at least I was where I wanted to be. If I couldn't have Mark, I could finally be back making sorrel soup. Take 4 cups of washed sorrel and cut off the stems carefully. (If you don't, the soup will be hairy, and no one will know it's the sorrel's hair and not the cook's.) Sauté the sorrel in 4 tablespoons butter until wilted. Add 2½ quarts chicken stock and 4 chopped peeled potatoes. Cook 45 minutes until potatoes are tender. Purée in a blender and add salt, pepper and hot red pepper flakes. Chill and add more salt and the juice of 1 lemon and 1 cup heavy cream. Serve with lemon slices.

The next morning the doorbell rang. I'd been up all night waiting for Mark to turn up to say it was all a terrible mistake, he really loved me, he must have been crazy, he didn't know what had gotten into him, and he would never see Thelma again if I would just come back to Washington immediately. I flung open the door to tell him I never wanted to see him again but I might consider coming back under certain circumstances, and who should it be but Jonathan Rice, the undersecretary of state and my partner in cuckoldom. I burst into tears and we fell into each other's arms.

"Oh, Jonathan," I said, "isn't it awful?"

"It's awful," he said. "What's happening to this country?" (Jonathan never takes anything personally; he always sees himself as a statistical reflection of a larger trend in society.)

Sam toddled into the living room and began methodically removing the books from the bookshelves, and Jonathan and I sat down and started on vodka mixed with Red Cheek apple juice. It turned out that Jonathan had been up half the night discussing the situation with Thelma and Mark, and when he realized neither of them was going to do a thing about it, he'd hopped on the shuttle and come to my father's, where Mark said I probably was.

"I had to talk to you," Jonathan said. "I love my wife." I'll skip the direct quotes, because it's too sickening—in less than twenty-four hours I'd had to listen to two grown men talking like saps about Thelma. He loved Thelma, Jonathan said, he had never loved anyone but Thelma, he had loved Thelma for nineteen years and would always love her even though Thelma didn't give a rat's ass about him and never had. She was a hysteric, Jonathan said, and a hopeless romantic; he'd been through this half a dozen times with her other men—the worst, he said, had been her affair with the undersecretary of the Nationalist Chinese embassy; she'd nearly had a nervous breakdown when Nixon recognized China and the Nationalists had to leave the country. "She got into bed and stayed there for weeks," said Jonathan. "Imagine my dilemma: there I was, on the Asia desk." He sighed. "Of course, normalization was psychologically hard on many Americans."

Still, Jonathan went on, he'd never seen Thelma quite so smitten with anyone as she was with Mark, and vice versa, and off went Jonathan on a long description of the presents Mark had given Thelma and the restaurants he'd taken her to and the meals they'd ordered and the business trips she'd gone along with him on and the hotels they'd stayed in and the room service (room service! he'd even had room service with her!) and the flowers that had arrived the next day. Just thinking about the flowers made me want to die, just thinking about the flowers he'd sent her while occasionally bringing me home a bunch of wilted zinnias. Mark is such a campaigner; he never just *does* something, he crusades for it. To realize, as I was suddenly beginning to realize, that all his energy had been going into Thelma Rice for all these months made me so sad I could hardly breathe. Jonathan went rattling on, pouring on detail after detail, to the point that I accused him of bugging his own telephone—he knew so much, he knew actual dialogue—but he claimed that Thelma simply told him everything. "We have an honest marriage," Jonathan said, and he glared at me as if I were somehow responsible for this whole mess because my marriage was so hopelessly dishonest. For months I'd been doing nothing but boiling eggs and teaching my child to differentiate between the cat in the hat and the fox in socks, and Jonathan Rice, the undersecretary of state, was actually angry at *me!* It's stuff like this that got us into Cambodia. Anyway, since Jonathan knew so much, I asked him if he happened to know exactly what it was that Mark and Thelma had been doing four days earlier, on the day the inscription in the children's book was dated. *I wanted to give you something to mark what happened today, which makes our future so much clearer. . . .* And of course he knew; the man knew everything. Four days earlier, my husband, Mark Feldman, had taken his paramour, Thelma Rice, to the Bloomingdale's furniture department, where they had looked at couches for his office. Bloomingdale's! The ultimate perfidy!

"But his office has a couch," I said.

"His *new* office," Jonathan said.

"What new office?" I said.

"The new office he wants to rent on Connecticut Avenue," said Jonathan. "And of course it needs a couch." He paused for emphasis. "You can't have a love nest without a couch." He paused again. "A convertible couch."

"I know I'm slow," I said, "but I did manage to figure the convertible part out."

The couch Thelma liked was green, Jonathan said, but Mark liked a brown tweed one, and they almost compromised on a pale yellow one but Thelma thought it would show the dirt, and just when I was becoming really sorry I'd asked, Jonathan came to the point— there was a point to his visit, it turned out— and said that he believed that if I came back to Mark, the two of us could wait the two of them out. He'd talked to the Guatemalan whiz-bang, he said—that's when I found out all three of them were seeing her—and she'd assured him that Mark's affair with Thelma would never last, because Mark had too much Jewish guilt and would never give up his children.

"Also," said Jonathan, "there's a lot Mark doesn't know about Thelma, and when he finds it out I'm sure he won't love her anymore."

"There's a lot Thelma doesn't know about Mark, too," I said.

"Like what?" said Jonathan.

"It doesn't matter," I said. "You know all this awful stuff about Thelma and you still love her, and I know all this awful stuff about Mark and I still love him, so what makes you think they're going to stop loving each other when they find out what we know about them?"

"Tell me some awful stuff about Mark," said Jonathan.

I couldn't think of much. Mark has to be reminded to clean his nails, and sometimes he says he's read a book when he's read only the first fifty pages of it, and he doesn't visit his Great-Aunt Minnie in the Hebrew Home as much as he should, but the truth is that the only really awful thing I knew about Mark Feldman was that he had betrayed me. That was a terrible thing, I don't mean to downplay it, but it wasn't the sort of thing Jonathan was looking for; Jonathan wanted to be told that Mark was a notorious plagiarist, or a shoplifter, or a scofflaw, and then he wanted to take the information home to Thelma like an old bone. Poor Jonathan. Poor pathetic doggie. The man actually believed he was going to argue her out of it. On top of everything else (not that I was going to tell him, although Thelma undoubtedly already had), Jonathan was up against a real piece of work in the sack, and it's hard to compete with that if you're the spouse who's been around for years; it's hard to compete with *anyone* new in the sack if you're the spouse who's been around for years. I really wanted to say something consoling to Jonathan, but every time the urge came over me to do so, he would drop one more piece of the betrayal into my lap: he was like a six-year-old boy who comes up to you with a shy smile, takes your hand and gently presses a snake into it. No wonder Thelma had fallen in love with Mark; if I'd spent nineteen years with Jonathan Rice, I would have run off with a delivery boy from the Fleet Messenger Service.

"I'm not going back to Mark," I said. "I'm not going to sit there while the two of them go on seeing each other on their convertible couch. I'm not going to wait this out."

"You're my only hope," Jonathan said.

I started crying again, and Jonathan put his arms around me and began muttering something about how the economy was in bad shape too, and there we were, hugging each other while Jonathan went on about the gross national product, when my father walked into the living room. He'd escaped from the loony bin in a jogging outfit.

"I'd like you to meet Jonathan Rice," I said.

"You're doing this in front of the kid?" said my father.

"It's not what you think," I said. "Mark is in love with Jonathan's wife."

"Who's Mark?" said my father.

"My husband," I said.

"It's the Thorazine talking," said my father. "They shoot you up with so much of it you can't even remember your son-in-law's name. Who was Charlie?"

"My first husband," I said.

"He's a fool," said my father.

"I thought you liked Charlie," I said.

"Not Charlie. Mark. Mark's a fool."

"What am I going to do?" I said. I started to sob. My father gave a little nod to Jonathan Rice, a little move-over-Buster-you're-in-the-way nod, and Jonathan untangled himself and stood up and my father sat down and tangled himself, and I shook and heaved and wheezed and snorted all over his sweatsuit. My father said a lot of terrific daddy things to me that made me cry even harder, partly because the dialogue was completely lifted from an obscure Dan Dailey movie he'd played a pediatrician in, and partly because he nevertheless delivered the lines so very well.

"What am I going to do?" I said.

"There's nothing you can do, baby," said my father.

"Of course there's something she can do," said Jonathan. "She can come back to him. If we both stick with it, we can sit this thing out."

"Jonathan is the undersecretary of state in charge of Middle Eastern affairs," I said.

My father looked at Jonathan. "I suppose they don't give that job to Jews," he said.

"That's right," said Jonathan.

"You want to make a pact with someone," said my father, "go call up the president of Egypt. Leave Rachel out of this." Then he told Jonathan to have a nice flight back and showed him to the door. Then he telephoned Lucy Mae Hopkins, the maid, and asked her to move into the apartment for a while to help take care of Sam. Then he called the Chinese restaurant down the block and ordered shrimp fried rice, which is something I love to eat when I'm feeling blue, shrimp fried rice with Chinese mustard and ketchup. Then, after Lucy Mae and the Chinese food arrived, he announced that he was going back to the loony bin because there wasn't room for all of us to sleep in the apartment.

"Men," he said as he left. "I hate them. I've always hated them. You wonder why I always hang around with women and never with men, it's because men do things like this." He waved his hand vaguely at me and my stomach, and jogged off into the night.

Of course, I knew he wasn't going back to the loony bin at all; he was going to see Frances. Frances is my father's mistress. She works at a paper company, and she has remained true to my father even though he keeps marrying other women and leaving her with nothing but commissions on his stationery orders. He orders an enormous amount of stationery, partly to keep a hand in with Frances, partly to have plenty of pieces of paper on which to write to me and my sister Eleanor about his will. Two or three times a month, my father threatens to cut me out of his will, and then he changes his mind, and each of these developments requires a letter. He also writes a lot of letters to Frances, promising that he'll end up with her eventually; I know this because once he accidentally put a letter to her into an envelope to me and vice versa. Frances got very excited when she opened the letter meant for me, because it had no salutation and she thought he was cutting *her* out of his will, which she hadn't realized she'd been written into in the first place. Why she puts up with him I don't know. Why any of us puts up with him I don't know. The truth is that if my father weren't my father, he would be one of the men he hates; he is incorrigibly faithless and thoroughly narcissistic, to such an extent that I tend to forget he's also capable of being a real peach.

(Another thing I like to eat when I'm feeling

blue is bacon hash. Cut some bacon into small pieces and start to cook it over a slow flame so that some of the fat is rendered. Then add diced cooked potatoes and cook slowly until the potatoes and bacon are completely crunchy. Eat with an egg.)

IV

*T*he shock of catapulting from the peanut-butter-and-jellyness of my life into High Drama was so great that the first morning I woke up, I was honestly stunned to discover it wasn't all a bad dream. That's a hopelessly banal metaphor, but that's just what it felt like, one of those bad dreams in which you realize you're having a bad dream and then you wake up in the dream to the same old bad dream—the dream equivalent of the cereal box with the baby on it eating breakfast next to the cereal box with the baby on it eating breakfast, forever and ever.

By the second morning, I'd given up on that. I woke up and lay there, watching the baby inside me make waves on my belly, and wondered what would become of me. Mark would turn up eventually, of course—but what if he didn't? What would I do? Where would I live? How much money would I need? Who would sleep with me? This last question interested me deeply, because I couldn't imagine that I'd ever be my normal shape again. I will be seven months pregnant forever, I thought, as the tears started to drip slowly into my ears, and after that I will be eight months pregnant forever, and after that I will be nine months pregnant forever. The only men I'd have a shot at would have to be used to thoroughly misshapen women, and that pretty much ruled out everyone but doctors. Under other circumstances, doctors would never have crossed my mind. I went out with one when I was in college. I was suffering from a finger that got abscessed when I stuck a ballpoint pen into a hangnail. He took one look at it and said, "Abscesses. Diabetes." This terrified me, because it's always seemed to me that there's a lot of diabetes among Jews, even though it's hard to pin anyone down on the question. Once, in fact, I tried to; I met a diabetes specialist, and I said to him, "May I ask you a question?"

He replied: "You want to ask me if Jews have more diabetes than anyone else."

"Yes," I said.

"Everyone asks me that," he said. "They don't. There's a sect in India that has more diabetes than Jews."

This reminded me of those feminists who are always claiming that male domination is

not the natural state because there's one tribe
in New Guinea where the men lie around
weaving and the women hunt bears. Anyway,
I didn't have diabetes, I merely had an abscessed finger. I have never since been remotely interested in doctors. But who else
would bother with me? There I was, seven
months gone, swaybacked, awkward, bloated,
logy, with a belly button that looked like a
pumpkin stem and feet that felt like old cu-
cumbers. If pregnancy were a book, they
would cut the last two chapters. The beginning is glorious, especially if you're lucky
enough not to have morning sickness and if,
like me, you've had small breasts all your life.
Suddenly they begin to grow, and you've got
them, you've really got them, breasts, darling
breasts, and when you walk down the street
they bounce, truly they do, they bounce
bounce bounce. You find yourself staring in
the mirror for long stretches of time, playing
with them, cupping them in your hands, push-
ing them this way and that, making cleavage,
making cleavage vanish, standing sideways,
leaning over, sticking them out as far as
they'll go, breasts, fantastic tender apricot
breasts, then charming plucky firm tange-
rines, and then, just as you were on the verge
of peaches, oranges, grapefruit, cantaloupes,
God knows what other blue-ribbon county-fair
specimens, your stomach starts to grow, and
the other fruits are suddenly irrelevant because they're outdistanced by an honest-to-

God watermelon. You look more idiotically out of proportion than ever in your life. You feel such nostalgia for the scrawny, imperfect body you left behind; and the commonsense knowledge that you will eventually end up shaped approximately the way you began is all but obliterated by the discomfort of not being able to sleep on your stomach and of peeing ever so slightly every time you cough and of leaking droplets from your breasts onto your good silk blouses and of suddenly finding yourself expert in mysteries you hadn't expected to comprehend until middle age, mysteries like swollen feet, varicose veins, neuritis, neuralgia, acid indigestion and heartburn.

Heartburn. That, it seemed to me as I lay in bed, was what I was suffering from. That summed up the whole mess: heartburn. Compound heartburn. Double-digit heartburn. Terminal heartburn. The tears poured from my eyes as I lit on the image, and the only thing that might have made it even more satisfyingly melodramatic and masochistic would have been to be lying in the bathtub; nothing like crying in the tub for real self-pity, nothing like the moment when every last bit of you is wet, and wiping the tears from your eyes only means making your face even wetter.

I considered staying in bed all day. I considered getting out of bed and into the bathtub and staying *there* all day. I wondered if even

considering these two alternatives constitut-
ed a nervous breakdown. (Probably not, I
decided.) I contemplated suicide. Every so
often I contemplate suicide merely to remind
myself of my complete lack of interest in it as
a solution to anything at all. There was a time
when I worried about this, when I thought
galloping neurosis was wildly romantic, when
I longed to be the sort of girl who knew the
names of wildflowers and fed baby birds with
eyedroppers and rescued bugs from swimming pools and wanted from time to time to
end it all. Now, in my golden years, I have
come to accept the fact that there is not a
neurasthenic drop of blood in my body, and I
have become very impatient with it in others.
Show me a woman who cries when the trees
lose their leaves in autumn and I'll show you
a real asshole.

I picked up the remote control unit and
turned on the television set. There was Phil
Donahue. He was interviewing five lesbians,
who had chosen the occasion of their appear-
ance on Donahue to come out of the closet. I
could just imagine the five of them, waiting through the years for the right offer, turning down Merv, turning down Kup, turning
down Cavett, watching contemptuously as
their friends chose mundane occasions like
Thanksgiving with Mom and Dad for the big
revelation, waiting for the big one, Phil himself, to finally come clean. I contemplated

lesbianism. Lesbianism has always seemed to me an extremely inventive response to the shortage of men, but otherwise not worth the trouble. It occurred to me that if I stayed in bed much longer, I would be forced to watch a soap opera. That seemed redundant, so I got up and went to group.

Under normal circumstances, I probably wouldn't mention my group. There's a real problem in dragging a group into a book: you have to introduce six new characters, bang bang bang, six new characters who are never going to be mentioned again in any essential way but who nonetheless have to be sketched in, simply because I can't really leave out of this story what happened to my group. Maybe you remember reading about it, I don't know. You'd probably remember if you did—because Vanessa Melhado is in my group. The advantage of having Vanessa Melhado in my group is that at least I don't have to introduce all six patients, since you've seen at least one of them in the movies. The other patients I'm going to have to describe by first name only: one of the many rules of group therapy is that you're not to know anyone's last name. With Vanessa, of course, you can't help knowing, she's too famous; and when my books started being published, everyone in the group learned mine; but until we all ended up on the front page together, we never knew anyone else's.

I hadn't been to my group in two years; when I moved to Washington, I'd graduated. The group held a special session in my honor, and it was really quite lovely. Everyone managed to say nice things to me except Diana, and I managed to say nice things to everyone except Diana, and Eve brought *grieven*, which are pieces of rendered chicken fat cooked with onions, and Ellis brought champagne, and even Dan, who never brings food and when he does it's only a tiny little container of cole slaw that doesn't go around, even Dan brought a cheesecake I'd given him the recipe for.

I got the cheesecake recipe from my father's second wife, Amelia, who was my family's housekeeper for years before she married him. Amelia, in fact, was what people were referring to when they said my mother was so gifted at Keeping Help. She was black—high yellow, to be exact—and ample (I think ample would be a polite way of describing her size) and covered with so many moles that she looked like a poppy seed cookie. And although it was clear that my father married her mostly to get even with my mother for marrying the Mel who thought he was God, it was still pretty inexcusable as these things went. What made it inexcusable, as far as I was concerned, was not that she was black and fat and looked like a poppy seed cookie, but that my father, in marrying her, got her to do for nothing exactly what she had been doing for a rather pleasant salary; this, it seemed to me, was going too far in the Keeping Help department. What made it inexcusable as far as my sister Eleanor was concerned was that she was sure Amelia was after my father's fortune. Since the Mel who thought he was God had already bankrupted my mother, Eleanor was positive the other half of the Tampax money would vanish as well and end up invested heavily in Amelia's only vice: wigs. "She's got at least forty of them now," Eleanor would say. "Imagine how many she'll have after he's gone."

Once I tried to engage Eleanor on the question of whether Amelia and my father had ever slept together, but she was in such a rage about the marriage there was really no dealing with her; she couldn't even enjoy empty speculation about it. Which was a shame, because Amelia was much too good-hearted to have been a gold digger, and she made my father happy, which is more than I can say of Eleanor and me, who were busy leading our own lives. Amelia cooked my father perfect meals and then sat down and giggled merrily at everything he said. In fact, she giggled merrily at everything everyone said. This put the burden of being amusing on whoever was with her, but my father loved it. My father occasionally says things like "A flying nun covers a multitude of sins" and then looks for a laugh, and it was a great comfort to him that Amelia was always good for one even if everyone else in the room was trying to ignore him.

What a cook she was! Everything she made was the lightest, the flakiest, the tenderest, the creamiest, the whateverest. She would stand at the kitchen counter—kneading dough for yeast rolls, making curls from carrots, rolling butter into balls—and tell me her secrets. She knew the mystery of my grandmother's cookies (sour cream), and she insisted there was only one true road to piecrust (Crisco). She had burn scars from her fingertips to her elbows, and she could tick them off: this one from a chicken fry for her mother's ninetieth birthday, this one from the first time she made potato pancakes, this one from a cast-iron pot she'd tended over a fire when she was growing up in the bayou. I owe her a huge debt—and her ending up with a big chunk of my father's money and a roomful of wigs would have been fine with me. But Amelia died after a year of marriage, and the only thing she ever got out of my father was a very nice grave somewhere in Louisiana.

Here's Amelia's cheesecake recipe; she always said she got it from the back of the Philadelphia cream cheese package. Make a nice graham cracker crust and pack it into a 9-inch pie pan. Then mix 12 ounces cream cheese with 4 well-beaten eggs, 1 cup sugar and a teaspoon vanilla. Pour into the pie shell and bake 45 minutes at 350°. Remove and cool 15 minutes. Then spread gently with 2 cups sour cream mixed with ½ cup sugar and bake 10 minutes more. Cool and refrigerate several hours before serving.

I took the subway to group. I always took the subway to and from Vera's; it cleared my head. I sat down, remembered to twist my diamond ring inward so the muggers wouldn't see it, and tried to concentrate on how I was going to tell the group what had happened to me. I felt mortified. Two years earlier, I had walked off into the sunset—cured! it's a miracle! she can walk!—and now I was back again, a hopeless cripple. I looked around the subway car. A Japanese man was taking pictures of the passengers. He was undoubtedly a tourist, but he was making everyone in the car uncomfortable. I tried not to look at him, but it was impossible. Once I saw an exhibitionist on the subway, and I tried not to look at him, too, but the funny thing about exhibitionists—and the reason I'm never really offended by them—is that you can't help sneaking a peek now and then to see if the damned thing is still sticking out. I looked at the Japanese man in a way that I hoped implied that I didn't really care if he took my picture, and that if he did take my picture I didn't really care that he was shooting my bad side, but then I decided I did care. So I smiled.

I look much better when I smile. In fact, when I don't smile, I look as if I'm frowning even though I'm not.

The Japanese man took my picture and nodded his head to me in a grateful fashion. I nodded back, and a man in a plaid shirt sitting next to me looked at me and winked. I immediately wondered whether he was single, and if so, whether he was a college graduate and straight. Then I thought of how awful it would be to be single again, how awful to be back on the market with the old New York ratio going against me, two hundred single women to every straight single man, packs of Amazons roaming the streets looking in vain for someone genuinely eligible and self-supporting who didn't mind a little cellulite. It was such a depressing thought that I almost began to cry—but then I remembered the Japanese man with the camera. I did not want anyone, even a stranger on the subway, to take a picture of me crying.

The man in the plaid shirt winked again, and I realized that even if he was single and a college graduate and straight, the odds were unlikely that I would ever get involved with an indiscriminate winker at pregnant women on subways. Anyone who winks at pregnant women on subways must have something wrong with him, it seemed to me. Of course, everyone has *something* wrong with him, that's for sure, but this guy probably had something *really* wrong. Perhaps he's a rapist, I thought, or a mugger. I figured that in my present physical condition I was fairly safe from rapists, but in case he was a mugger and knew how to recognize a diamond ring even when it was turned inward, I twisted the ring off in what I hoped was a thoroughly discreet manner, made an ambiguous gesture as if I were pulling at the skin on my throat, and cleverly dropped the ring into my bra.

The subway came to Union Square and I got out. There was Ellis. Ellis is in my group. He was buying popcorn at the nut stand in the subway station, and when he saw me he looked so pleased that he threw the entire contents of the box of popcorn over his head, and just stood there grinning as it settled onto and around him. He was like a living version of a snowman in a glass ball you shake the snow inside of. I was glad to see him, too, but I couldn't tell him that because another rule of group is that members are not allowed to have conversations of any sort outside the group room, so we walked together without saying a word all the way to Vera's office.

Vera was sitting at the low, round table, opening the containers of food the group members had brought for lunch. Vanessa was there, and Eve and Diana and Sidney and Dan—and they clucked over the photographs of Sam and asked when the new baby was due and looked truly horrified when I told them why I was there.

"My husband is in love with someone else"

is hard to say flat out. "My husband thinks he's in love with someone else" is as close as I came before bursting into tears. Even Diana looked truly horrified, which surprised me because Diana always gets a little smile on her face when something awful happens to me. Years earlier, I had come into group one day and burst into tears, and Diana had gotten that little smile on her face; she was really disappointed to discover that the reason I was crying was that I'd been assaulted by a cabdriver; no doubt she'd been hoping for a more personal tragedy, with longer-lasting effects. Well, now she had one.

Sidney handed me a box of Kleenex. Sidney never really says much in group—he just passes the Kleenex and looks solicitous. I wiped my eyes and managed to stop sobbing long enough to get most of the story out. Then I burst into tears again, and so did Diana.

"Why does everything happen to Rachel and nothing ever happens to me?" she cried.

"Stick it up your ass, Diana," said Ellis.

"You'd like to, wouldn't you?" said Diana. "That's the only way you like it, I bet."

"I like it all ways, which is more than I can say for your husband," said Ellis.

"Who brought the chopped liver?" asked Dan.

"I did," said Eve.

"Did you make it?" asked Dan.

"I bought it," said Eve. "Is that all right with you?"

"I was about to tell you it was delicious," said Dan. "Now I don't feel like telling you."

"Nothing's ever enough for you, is it?" said Eve.

"Every week you complain about the food," said Vanessa. "When's the last time *you* brought food to group? When's the last time you brought anything to group?"

"What did I do now?" said Dan.

"What did you do *now*?" said Eve.

"You know what this reminds me of?" said Vera.

"The old woman from Vladivostok and the camel," said Ellis.

"Please don't tell that one again," said Vanessa.

"I won't," said Vera. "But that isn't even the point. Why don't you want to talk about Rachel?"

"I'm too threatened to talk about Rachel," said Eve. "I believe in Rachel. I believe in Rachel and Mark. If they can't make it, who can?"

"Vera and Niccolo," said Ellis.

"They don't count," said Vanessa.

Everyone nodded glumly.

"Who's the other woman?" said Diana.

"It doesn't matter," I said.

"It matters to Diana," said Ellis. "All Diana cares about is finding out people's last names."

I told them a little about Thelma. I said she had a nose as long as a thumb and walked like a penguin; that made me feel better. I said Mark was a schmuck; that made me feel even better. I told the part about all three of them going to see the Central American therapist and her dwarf dog, and I said how unfair it was that I couldn't even date.

"She must be feeling better," said Ellis. "She's making jokes."

"She makes jokes even when she's feeling terrible," said Vera. "Don't let her fool you."

"Why do you have to make everything into a joke?" asked Diana.

"I don't have to make everything into a joke," I said. "I have to make everything into a story. Remember?"

"How do you feel?" asked Eve.

"Hurt. Angry. Stupid. Miserable." I thought for a minute. "And guilty."

"You didn't do this," said Eve. "*He* did."

"But I picked him," I said.

"Anyone would have picked Mark Feldman," said Vanessa.

"No last names in group," said Vera.

"Anyway, it's not over," said Eve. "He'll be back."

"And then what?" I said. "It's like a beautiful thing that suddenly turns out to be broken into hundreds of pieces, and even when you glue it back together it's always going to have been horribly broken."

"That's what a marriage is," said Sidney. "Pieces break off, and you glue them back on."

"Look at it this way," said Vanessa, "it's not a total loss. At least you got Sidney to say something."

Sidney looked quite pleased with himself.

"Are you done, Sidney?" asked Ellis.

"Yes," said Sidney.

"Because if you are," said Ellis, "I just want to say that I don't think that's what a marriage is."

"That *is* what a marriage is," said Dan. "After a certain point it's just patch, patch, patch."

"That's not what Vera and Niccolo's marriage is," said Eve.

Everyone nodded glumly again.

"Sometimes I wish you and Niccolo would get a divorce," I said to Vera. "Your marriage is very hard on the rest of us."

"I saw Niccolo last week," said Vanessa, "and he told me that occasionally at the end of the day he and Vera get irritable with each other."

"I would kill for merely irritable," I said.

"Under what circumstances did you see Niccolo last week?" Diana asked.

"He and Vera came to a screening of my new movie," said Vanessa.

"And when you become a movie star, Diana, I'll come to a screening of your new movie, too," said Vera.

"Thanks a lot," said Diana. Diana is a computer programmer.

"What do you want?" said Vanessa. "Mark

is going to turn up, and you have to know what you want when he does."

I thought about it.

"I want him back," I said.

"What do you want him back for?" said Dan. "You just said he was a schmuck."

"I want him back so I can yell at him and tell him he's a schmuck," I said. "Anyway, he's my schmuck." I paused. "And I want him to stop seeing her. I want him to say he never really loved her. I want him to say he must have been crazy. I want her to die. I want him to die, too."

"I thought you said you wanted him back," said Ellis.

"I do," I said, "but I want him back dead."

I smiled. It was the first time I'd smiled about the situation. I looked around the room, expecting everyone to be smiling back, but they were all looking in my direction as if something strange was going on. Ellis was the first to speak. "You haven't by any chance hired an assassin without telling us first, have you?"

I turned to look behind me. A man wearing a nylon stocking over his head was standing at the door, holding a snubnosed revolver. He grabbed me around the neck, pulled me to my feet, and pressed the gun against my temple. "On the table," he said. "Money, jewelry, anything you've got that I want. Hold anything back and I'll kill the lady just like this—" And for an instant, he aimed the gun at the wall, pulled the trigger and fired. Everyone jumped at the explosive crack and turned to watch a framed photograph of Theodor Reik break into shards and fall to the floor. A second later, a framed Chivas Regal ad with a caption that said "The bottle is either half empty or half full depending on how you look at it" fell off the wall, too.

"I always hated that picture," said Sidney.

"This is not the time to talk," said Vera.

She took off the strands of antique beads from around her neck, and her three lacy wedding bands, and put them into the middle of the table. Everyone started to throw money onto the pile. Vanessa unsnapped the gold necklace she'd been given after something (though not that much) had happened between her and John Wayne in Mexico. Diana made a great show of removing her plastic bracelets and throwing them ceremoniously into the taramasalata.

The man in the nylon stocking pressed the gun into my temple so hard that I almost cried out. I closed my eyes. "Your turn, lady," he said.

I could feel the diamond ring I had slipped into my bra pressing against my breast. Mark had given me the ring when Sam was born. We had gotten to the hospital when the contractions were coming only five minutes apart, and Mark sat in the labor room, next to me, holding my arm, whispering, singing, making little jokes, doing everything right. I'd

been absolutely positive that he wouldn't—
that he'd turn into the kind of hopeless father
who goes through the whole business under
the delusion that it's as much his experience
as it is yours. All this starts in Lamaze class-
es, where your husband ends up thinking he's
pregnant, and let me tell you he's not. It's not
his body, it's not his labor, it's not his pain—
it's yours, and does any man give you credit or
respect for it? No. They're too busy getting in
on the act, holding their stopwatches and
telling you when to breathe and when to push
and taking pictures of the kid coming out all
covered with goo and showing them to your
friends at dinner parties and saying what a
beautiful and moving experience it was. Not
Mark. He just sat there helping me to get
through, and he stayed completely calm when
the doctor said there was something wrong,
perhaps the umbilical cord was around the
baby's neck; and he looked so impassive when
he glanced over at the fetal monitor and saw
that the baby had stopped breathing that I
didn't even realize how serious the situation
was; he just kept on whispering and singing
and making little jokes as they rushed me into
the operating room and knocked me out for
the emergency Caesarean.

When I came to, he was standing next to
me. He was wearing a green surgical smock
and a mask, and he was crying and laughing,
and in his arms was Sam, our beautiful Sam,
our sunray, pink and gold and cooing like a

tiny dove. Mark laid him on me, and then he lay down next to me on the narrow slab, and held us both until I fell asleep again.

Two hours later, when I woke up, he gave me the ring. He'd just gone out and bought it. The diamond was in an antique setting surrounded by tiny little diamonds; it looked like a delicate ice flower. The next day Mark took it back to the jeweler and had it engraved: "Rachel and Mark and Sam."

I've always wondered what I would have done about the diamond ring in my bra under other circumstances. If I'd had a choice. I didn't have a choice, because the man in the nylon stocking was the man in the plaid shirt, and he'd seen me put the ring in my bra on the subway. But suppose he hadn't? Would I have handed it over? Would I have risked my life to hold on to the ring? I don't know. All I know is that when the man in the plaid shirt and nylon stocking said, "Your turn, lady," he was gesturing toward my bra. So I reached into the bra and gave it to him. He motioned to Eve to put the other things into a bag, and she did.

"Now everyone lie down on the floor," he said. He kept the gun pressed against my head and began backing out of the room, holding me against him. "No one calls the police," he said. "Otherwise I hurt the lady." He opened the door to the hallway and took off the nylon stocking. We got into the elevator and started down.

"I'm sorry about your ring," he said.

"Don't say things you don't mean," I said.

He stepped out into the vestibule and ran out the door of the building to the street. I rode back up and walked into Vera's office. Everyone stood up, looking a little embarrassed, and Vera went to call the police. There was a lot of hugging while she was out of the room. Hugging is against the rules, too, but so is robbery, so no one cared.

"They'll be here in a few minutes," Vera said when she came back. She looked around the room. "You must all feel that I failed to protect you."

"Don't blame Vera," I said. "It was my fault."

"You always think it's your fault," said Vanessa. "You're much too guilty."

"Can't anything ever be Rachel's fault?" asked Diana.

"He saw me on the subway," I said. "He saw me take my ring off and stick it into my bra. He must have followed me here, only I was walking with Ellis so he couldn't rob me on the way."

"I hope you and Ellis weren't having a conversation outside the group room," said Dan.

"We weren't," said Ellis, "but if we had been, we probably would have been talking about what a creep you are."

There was a long silence.

"This is going to get into the papers," said

Vanessa. "That's going to be my fault." Everything Vanessa did ended up in the papers.

"Good," said Diana. "We're going to find out everyone's last names."

"I have something terrible to say," said Ellis. "I was attracted to him." He looked thoroughly ashamed of himself. "He had a nylon stocking over his face and I was attracted to him."

"I saw him without the nylon stocking," I said.

"And?" said Ellis.

"And I was attracted to him, too."

"But you're desperate," said Ellis.

"That's true," I said. "But don't rub it in."

V

*O*ne afternoon, some months before all this happened, I was working in the kitchen in our house in Washington trying to perfect my system for a four-minute egg. Here's how you make a four-minute egg: Put an egg into cold water and bring it to the boil. Turn off the heat immediately and put the lid on the saucepan. Let it sit. In three minutes, you will have a perfect four-minute egg. It just so happens that the world is not waiting breathlessly for a three-minute way to make a four-minute egg, but sometimes, when you are a food person, the possible irrelevance of what you are doing doesn't cross your mind until it's too late. (Once, for example, when I was just starting out in the food business, I was hired by the caper people to develop a lot of recipes using capers, and it was weeks of tossing capers into just about everything but milkshakes before I came to terms with the fact that nobody really likes capers no matter what you do with them. Some people *pretend* to like capers, but the truth is that any dish that tastes good with capers in it tastes even better with capers not in it.)

Anyway, there I was, boiling eggs at three-twenty on a Thursday afternoon. I know the exact time, because I looked at the clock as soon as I heard the shout. A man was shouting —screaming, actually. A fight, I thought. A terrible fight, I thought. A fight so terrible that someone is going to get killed, I thought. I went to the front door and opened it. The shouting stopped. I went back to the eggs. That evening, when Mark came home, I said, "If someone was murdered on this block this afternoon, it happened at three-twenty." Mark paid no attention at all. At the time I thought this was because he thought I was turning into the sort of melodramatic woman who is forced to imagine excitement and romance and intrigue because she's stuck at home all day; but I realize now that his affair with Thelma was just beginning, and his reaction was simply the one you affect when you're becoming involved with someone else and you're determined not to be remotely interested in or amused or touched by the person you're married to.

Now that I think about it, perhaps I *was* turning into a certain kind of melodramatic woman—not the kind who fantasizes because she's housebound but the kind who's simply trying to get her husband's attention because she knows that he's somewhere else, with someone else. Even then, back when the affair was starting, mustn't I have had an inkling? I can't bear that I didn't, but that's not the reason I'm telling the story about the man down the block who was murdered, so I'll get back to it.

Three days later. A Sunday. Mark and I were on our way out to lunch. The police. A half-open door to the house across the street. On the floor of the foyer, a huge brownish stain. "If there's a dead body in there," I said to the policeman outside, "it happened at three-twenty on Thursday afternoon." There was. It was Mr. Abbey, a meek little man who had had his last fling with rough trade. And I was the only witness! I don't mean to get so excited here, but I've always wanted to be a witness. I've always wanted to swear to tell the truth, the whole truth, and nothing but the truth and spar with lawyers and be sketched by courtroom artists. Now my time had come! And I knew nothing. It really was depressing, and not just for me, but for the homicide detective on the case, who kept trying to pry information out of me.

"You know more than you think," Homicide Detective Hartman kept saying, as he urged me to search my memory for the additional details he was certain were buried there.

"No I don't," I said.

A few days after Mr. Abbey's body was discovered, Homicide Detective Hartman came back to take another crack at my subconscious. He was full of interesting information. He told me that Mr. Abbey had spent the last morning of his life at a furniture auction. Afterward, a friend who was there had asked him to lunch. Mr. Abbey refused. He said he had seen a beautiful black man cruising the bus terminal the night before, and was going back to find him. And that was the last anyone saw of Mr. Abbey.

I was fascinated by the story. I couldn't believe that anyone would be so sexually driven that he might actually skip lunch—and after an auction! I think of myself as a healthy person with a strong sex drive, but it's never occurred to me to forgo meals. I said this to Mark later. I said, perhaps this is the difference between homosexuals and heterosexuals, perhaps this relentless priapism is characteristic of the obsessive, casual sex that lasts so much later in the lives of homosexuals than in heterosexuals. And Mark got this look on his face, this incredulous look, that at the time I thought meant he couldn't believe I could have such a short memory. Had I forgotten the first months of our courtship? The hours and hours of sex, the smell of it everywhere, in the air, on the sheets, on my hands, in my hair—had I managed to forget all that? (Of course I hadn't; on the other hand, we never once had less than three meals a day, so there.) Now, of course, I know about Thelma, and I realize that Mark's incredulity arose simply because I knew so little about him and *his* relentless priapism, knew so little about *men*. When will I ever learn? When will I ever understand that what's astonishing about the number of men who remain faithful is not that it's so small but that there are any of them at all?

I see that once again I've gotten off the track, that I've drifted back to Mark, to Mark and Thelma, but I can't help myself. When something like this happens, you suddenly have no sense of reality at all. You have lost a piece of your past. The infidelity itself is small potatoes compared to the low-level brain damage that results when a whole chunk of your life turns out to have been completely different from what you thought it was. It becomes impossible to look back at anything that's happened—from the simplest exchange between the two of you at a dinner party to the horrible death of Mr. Abbey—without wondering what was really going on. See the couple. See the couple with the baby. See the couple with the baby having another baby. *What's wrong with this picture?* Everything, as it happens.

But I was telling you about Mr. Abbey's death for a reason, and it has nothing to do with betrayal. I simply wanted you to understand that when my group was robbed, I was almost grateful: it gave me another shot at being a witness to a crime. And this time I knew stuff, I really knew stuff. I had actually laid eyes on the bugger. I couldn't wait to be deposed, or whatever it is they call what they do to you.

They took us to the station house in a paddy wagon. This was fairly insulting, since we were the victims, but the detective in charge of the case had so many statements to take that he wanted to do it with stenographers and typewriters and tape recorders nearby. We spent the afternoon in a small green room and each waited his turn. First the police talked to Vera, because she was in charge of the premises, as they say, and then they talked to Vanessa, because she was the most famous and beautiful (I've come to terms with the fact that Vanessa is the most famous and beautiful, but it really irritated me that day since after all I was the one who knew the most about what happened), and then they talked to Diana because she insisted she would hold them responsible if she missed her Supersaver flight to Los Angeles. Finally Detective Nolan got to me.

I told him everything. I said the robber was about six feet tall. Sandy hair. Watery blue eyes. A little squint. Pinkish complexion. A long, thin nose on a wide, shiny face. Weighed about 165—I can never be sure what men weigh. A fat neck. A red and green plaid cotton shirt, a khaki jacket, jeans and running shoes. I first noticed him when a Japanese man on the subway took my picture. My guess is that the Japanese man has a picture of the robber.

"What did the Japanese man look like?" asked Detective Nolan.

"Japanese," I said. "You know."

"I know," said Detective Nolan. "Small and Oriental and wearing a dark gray suit, with a camera around his neck."

"Yes," I said.

"What kind of camera?"

I shrugged. "I thought I was doing pretty well till we got to this part," I said.

"You are doing very well," said Detective Nolan.

"You say that to everybody," I said.

"No I don't," he said.

"Yes you do," I said. "I was a witness to something else recently, and the detective kept telling me how well I was doing, but I wasn't really."

"What else were you a witness to?" said Detective Nolan.

"A murder in Washington," I said. "I wasn't actually a witness—I just heard the shouting. Why?"

"I just wondered," said Detective Nolan.

"You just wondered if I was the kind of woman who attracts criminals the way other women attract alcoholics or sadists." (I have a friend who attracts dwarfs. Every time she turns around, a dwarf is following her. It's very disturbing.)

"No," said Detective Nolan. "What made you notice the man on the subway?"

"He winked at me," I said.

"I see," said Detective Nolan.

"It was probably my fault," I said, "because I was smiling at the Japanese man, because I'd rather have my picture taken when I'm smiling because when I'm not smiling I look as if I'm frowning, and that's when the robber winked at me, so I wondered if he was single, and then he winked again and I wondered if he was a mugger, and that's when I put my diamond ring into my bra."

"You mean you just looked at him and automatically wondered if he was single?"

"Well, he winked at me," I said.

"What made you think he might be a mugger?"

"I didn't really *believe* he was a mugger," I said. "I just realized that he might not be a suitable object for fantasy. I didn't even know if he'd gone to college."

"Are you sure there wasn't some detail you can't quite remember that alerted you in some way?"

"Like the bulge of his revolver under his jacket?" I said.

"Yes," said Detective Nolan.

"I don't think so," I said, "but it's possible that he was looking at my ring before I twisted it backwards, and I knew that. Subconsciously, I mean."

"Subconsciously," said Detective Nolan.

"I just remembered something," I said. "The Japanese man was wearing a little identification card. The kind they give you at conventions."

"Excellent," said Detective Nolan, and left the room. A few minutes later he came back and sat down.

"How long do you think it would take me?" he said.

"To find the Japanese man?" I said.

"To have therapy," he said. "How long would it take?"

"What's wrong with you?" I said.

"Nothing much," he said.

"Nine years," I said.

"How long did it take you?" he said.

"Nine years," I said. "Of course, I've had two years off for good behavior, but now I'm back. And there was nothing much wrong with me, either. That's why I graduated in the first place. The ones there's really something wrong with are in forever."

"Why did you start nine years ago?" asked Detective Nolan.

"I wanted a divorce," I said.

"From this guy who's being so terrible to you now?"

"From the first one," I said. I looked at him. "Diana told you, didn't she? I know she did. That bitch."

"I'm sorry to bring it up," said Detective Nolan. "It's not even relevant. Although it might explain why you were wondering whether the guy on the subway was single."

"That's true," I said.

"I was thinking of going into therapy because I can't decide whether to have a hair transplant," said Detective Nolan.

"You already have an awful lot of hair," I said.

"It's not mine," said Detective Nolan.

"It looks pretty good," I said.

"You think so?" he said.

"Yes," I said.

"I'm just telling you that so you know something about me, and since I know something about you, we're even."

"I don't think you need therapy," I said. "You might be the only person in America who doesn't."

I finished being interviewed by Detective Nolan, and gave him my father's telephone number and my number at home in Washington just in case. It wasn't until I was past the newspaper photographers and on the subway that I wondered whether Detective Nolan was single. He wasn't exactly my type, but look where my type had gotten me. Then I wondered if he was uncircumcised. Then I wondered if I could be happily married to a policeman. Then I wondered why I was so hopelessly bourgeois that I couldn't even have a fantasy about a man without moving

on to marriage. Then I stopped wondering.
For one thing, the subway arrived at my stop
and I got off. For another, it seemed clear to
me that it would never matter. When I got to
my father's apartment, I was sure, Mark
would be there.

And he was.

VI

I met Mark Feldman at a party in Washington at my friend Betty's. Betty Searle and I went to college together, and we always used to talk about living together afterward; but one day Betty said that I was a brunette and belonged in New York and she was a blonde and belonged in Washington, and she was right. Betty went off to Washington and became famous for her local television show, her dinner parties, and her affairs with a first-rate cross section of the American left wing. Every Christmas she had a party that everyone in Washington came to, and there, one Christmas, was Mark. I recognized him the minute he walked in because I'd seen him on *Meet the Press*, and once you see that beard you never forget it. He has a black beard, but the part of it that's on the left side of his chin has a little white stripe in it, where the skin underneath has no pigment. Just like a skunk is what you're thinking, and you're right, but it can look very odd and interesting. I've always liked odd and interesting-looking men because I'm odd and interesting-looking myself, and I always figured I had a better shot at them than at the conventionally good-looking ones. (Water seeks its own level, et cetera.) My mother would have loved Mark Feldman's beard. "A scar but not" is what she would have called it.

Mark is a syndicated columnist, that's why I'd seen him on television. He writes about Washington as if it's a city like any other (it's not), filled with rich and interesting characters (it's not). He's known for being chronically perverse about politics. For instance, some people think it's terrible that Washington doesn't work, but Mark thinks it's wonderful, because if it worked, something might actually be accomplished and then we'd really be in bad shape. This is a very clever way of being cynical, but never mind.

"Stay away from him," Betty said, when she saw me looking over at him.

"Why?" I said.

"He's trouble," she said.

"Please don't throw me in the brier patch," I said.

So Mark Feldman and I went out to dinner. He told me the story of his first day in the newspaper business. I told him the story of wanting to play the ukulele in the school orchestra. And then we went to bed. We stayed there for about three weeks. Every so often he got up to write a column, and I got up to call my answering machine in New York to see if there was any reason not to be in Washington for a while longer. There wasn't.

At some point in those three weeks, we had gotten out of bed for some reason or other, and we were taking a walk near the Pension Building. It's a huge, block-square structure with a frieze of Civil War soldiers, thousands of soldiers moving cannons and guns and wagons and horses slowly around the perimeter of the building. We went up the stairs to the entrance, and the guard let us into the inner courtyard. It was barely lit. The guard went down the hall and turned on the lights, and suddenly I could see the huge open space in the center of the building, pillars three stories high, leaded glass at the top. For many years, the inaugural balls were held in the Pension Building. We could hear the guard's radio, with an old Sinatra song coming from it. Mark held out his hands.

"I can't dance," I said. "I've never been able to."

"I believe in you, Rachel," he said.

We started to dance.

"You didn't believe me," I said.

"I'm not going to step on your foot," Mark said.

"I know that," I said.

"No you don't," he said.

He stepped back and put his right hand on the front of his waist and his left hand on the back.

"Right here," he said. "That part of you is mine for the next three minutes. After that I'll give it back. But you have to give it to me for now."

"I have to trust you," I said.

"Right."

"I have to *follow* you," I said.

"Right."

"Oh, God," I said.

"You can do it, Rachel," he said, and he put his arms out again. We started to dance. I closed my eyes. And I relaxed. People are always telling me to relax—the hairdresser tells me to relax, and the dentist, and the exercise teacher, and the dozen or so tennis pros who have attempted to do something about my backhand—but the only time I think I've ever really relaxed in my entire life was for three minutes in the Pension Building dancing with Mark Feldman.

"I'm dancing," I said.

"I love you," he said.

So we were in love. We were madly in love. We flew back and forth on the Eastern shuttle and we called each other on various WATS lines and I became best friends with his best friends and he became best friends with my best friends, and there were presents and concerts and three-pound lobsters at the

Palm, and then one day I came down to Washington and walked into his apartment and found a Virginia Slim cigarette butt in an ashtray. *Who's been eating my porridge?* Mark said it was the maid's. I pointed out that the maid smoked Newports. Then he said it was his sister's. I pointed out that his sister had stopped smoking. Then he said he had bummed it from a copy girl at the office. I said that even copy girls at the office weren't naive enough to smoke Virginia Slims. Then he got angry and said if he'd wanted to live with a detective he'd live with a detective and why didn't I trust him? Then I got angry and said if he was going to bum cigarettes he ought to bum Marlboros so I wouldn't think he was cheating on me, and why didn't he at least have the decency to empty the ashtray into the garbage disposal.

Next thing you know, we were at a party—a party for his book about Washington—and I looked across the room and saw him talking to a reporter from the *Sydney Morning Herald*, and she started laughing, and even her laugh had an Australian accent. I walked over and carefully linked my arm through his. "Oh," she said, "Mark was just telling me the most amusing story about his first day in the newspaper business."

Then off he went on his book tour.

"Hi, I'm Irv Kupcinet, and my guests to-night are Mark Feldman, syndicated colum-nist and author of the new best-seller Return

to Power; *Toby Bright, director of the Insti-
tute of Sexual Analysis and herself the best-
selling author of* Good in Bed; *former British
Prime Minister Harold Wilson; and Graham
Kerr, the Galloping Gourmet, who is here
today to talk about Jesus Christ.*"

A couple of days after I saw the show on
television, I was having lunch with my friend
Marie, at the omelet place on Sixty-first
Street.

"I met Mark," Marie said.

"When?" I said.

"I was in Chicago a few days ago when he
was on his book tour."

"Where did you meet him?"

"*Playboy* had a party for some book."

"And?"

"He seemed nice," Marie said. "I couldn't
really tell that much. It was crowded and all."
She started playing with her ratatouille filling.

"Marie?"

"I keep thinking about it," Marie said. "You
know. If it were reversed, what would I want
you to do? What do you think?"

"I think it takes two people to hurt you," I
said. "The one who does it and the one who
tells you."

"I know," said Marie. "Shit."

"But I'd want you to tell me," I said. "Who
was she?"

"The one who wrote the sex book," said
Marie.

"They were together at the party," I said.

"And later," said Marie. "At the hotel."

"That bastard," I said.

"Look," said Marie, "he's got a big book, he's having a fling, it'll go away."

"Listen," I said. "I had a book. I did the Kup show. And I didn't fuck the Galloping Gourmet, and he wasn't into Jesus Christ then, either."

"I feel terrible," said Marie.

"Don't you dare steal feeling terrible from me," I said.

"This isn't fair," said Marie. "You're so much better at this than I am. You've been in group."

Of course, we could talk for days about why Marie told me. I'm glad she told me—it saved me from finding out at a later time—but still you have to wonder. Anyway, Mark and I broke up. I flew down to Washington and collected my things and had a big fight with Mark in which he accused me of the thing men think is the most insulting thing they can accuse you of—wanting to be married—and he took me to the airport and my duffel bag burst in the middle of the National Airport parking lot and all the whisks and frying pans and cookbooks fell out on the ground and then we had another big fight over whether it was his Julia Child or mine that I was taking back to New York (it was his) and that was that.

"Well, you knew he was trouble from the very beginning, didn't you?" said Vera after it was over. Which is the kind of thing Vera is always saying, and which I fundamentally agree with but nonetheless get extremely irritable about.

"Of course I knew that," I said. "I told it to you right after I met him. And you know what you said? You said, 'Everybody has a past.'"

"I never said that," said Vera.

"You certainly did say that," I said.

"What I said was that people are capable of change," said Vera. "If you don't think people can change, what are you doing here?"

"Investing my money in caftans," I said.

The telephone rang and Vera answered it. "What's the split on the paperback?" she said to whoever was calling. "What does your agent say?" She nodded. "Well, hold out for sixty-forty over two hundred fifty thousand." She hung up and looked at me.

"You think I picked Mark because I knew what was going to happen," I said.

"Did I say that?" said Vera.

"You don't have to say it, Vera."

"Well?" she said.

"No," I said. "No."

"An old man goes to buy a horse," said Vera. "Have I told you this story?"

"I can't tell yet," I said. "They all sound alike in the beginning."

"Goes to buy a horse," said Vera. "The horse trader says, 'I can sell you a very nice horse for five hundred rubles.' 'What else do you have?' says the old man. The horse trader

says, 'Well, for one hundred fifty rubles I can
sell you a donkey. He won't live as long, but
he'll get you from Kiev to Vilna.' The old man
buys the donkey, and two weeks later it drops
dead. So he goes back to the horse trader and
says, 'How was I to know?'"

"Is that a story about how smart you are, or
how dumb I am?" I said.

"Both," said Vera.

"Well, at least this time I get to be a person
in the story. The last time you told one of your
Russian parables I was a bag of chickens."

There was a long pause.

"Well?" said Vera.

"It's not as simple as that, Vera," I said.
"You want everything to be simple. You think
I'm just standing there, and this army of men
is walking by, shouting, 'Choose *me*, choose
me,' and I always pick the turkey. Life's not
like that. I can't even find a man who lives in
the same city I do."

"Of course you can," said Vera.

Well, of course I couldn't. The next man I
was involved with lived in Boston. He taught
me to cook mushrooms. He taught me that if
you heat the butter very hot and put just a
very few mushrooms into the frying pan, they
come out nice and brown and crispy, whereas
if the butter is only moderately hot and you
crowd the mushrooms, they get all mushy and
wet. Every time I make mushrooms I think of
him. There was another man in my life when
I was younger who taught me to put sour

cream into scrambled eggs, and since I never ever put sour cream into scrambled eggs I never really think of him at all.

Two months passed. I flew to Boston every other weekend. The man in Boston flew to New York every other weekend. I was deeply involved in piecrust. I was perfectly happy. And Mark turned up. Mark turned up full of repentance and bearing gifts. He sent flowers. He sent jewelry. He sent chocolates, and not those overly refined Swiss ones either—nice chewy, nutty American ones. He called up and said psychoanalytic things on the phone. He said he had made the worst mistake of his life and he wanted me back and he would love me forever and he would never hurt me again. He said he wanted to marry me. He said he was going to marry me. He said I might as well get used to the idea. He asked me to marry him on the IRT downtown local, and he asked me to marry him on the Forty-ninth Street crosstown bus. He asked me to marry him so often—and I refused so often—that when he failed to ask me for a day or so, I started to worry. He campaigned for me. He spoke of babies. Forever and ever. "Let's sing all the songs we know about marriage," he said to me one morning. Picture a little love nest, he sang, out where the roses cling. Picture the same sweet love nest, I sang back, think what a year can bring.

There were two reasons I didn't want to marry Mark. First of all, I didn't trust him.

And second of all, I'd already been married. Mark had already been married, too, but that didn't really count; it certainly didn't count in the way it usually counts, which is that it makes you never want to get married again. Mark's first wife was named Kimberly. (As he always said, she was the first Jewish Kimberly.) Mark and Kimberly were married for less than a year, but he had enough material from her to last a lifetime. "My wife, the first Jewish Kimberly," Mark would begin, "was so stingy that she made stew out of leftover pancakes." Or: "My wife, the first Jewish Kimberly, was so stingy she once tried to sell a used nylon stocking to a mugger." In truth, the first Jewish Kimberly really was stingy, she recycled everything, and she once blew up their apartment and most of what was in it while making brandy out of old cherry pits.

My first husband was stingy, too, but that was the least of it. My first husband was so neurotic that every time he had an appointment, he erased the record of it from his datebook, so that at the end of the year his calendar was completely blank. My first husband was so neurotic he kept hamsters. They all had cute names, like Arnold and Shirley, and he was very attached to them and was always whipping up little salads for them with his Slice-o-Matic and buying them extremely small sweaters at a pet boutique in Rego Park. My first husband was so neurotic he would never eat fish because he'd once choked on a fishbone, and he would never eat onions because he claimed he was allergic to them, which he wasn't. I know, because I snuck them into everything. You can't really cook without onions. "Is this an onion?" Charlie would say, his eyes narrowing as he held up a small, translucent object he had discovered floating in the sauce that covered his boneless dinner. "No, it's a celery," I would say. It didn't really fool him; at the end of every meal he would leave a neat little pile of small, translucent objects on his plate. God, was he neat. My first husband was so neat he put hospital corners on the newspaper he lined the hamster cage with.

The reason my marriage to Charlie broke up—although by now you're probably astonished that it lasted even a minute—was not because he slept with my oldest friend Brenda or even that he got crabs from her. It was because Arnold died. I felt really sad when Arnold died, because Charlie was devoted to Arnold and had invented a fairly elaborate personality for Arnold that Arnold did his best to live up to. Hamsters don't really do that much, but Charlie had built an entire character for Arnold and made up a lot of hamster jokes he claimed Arnold had come up with, mostly having to do with chopped lettuce. Also, and I'm sorry to tell you this, Charlie often talked in a high, squeaky voice that was meant to be Arnold's, and I'm even sorrier to tell you that I often replied in a high, squeaky voice that was meant to be Shirley's. You enter into a certain amount of madness when you marry a person with pets, but I didn't care. When Charlie and I were married, I was twenty-five years and eleven months old, and I was such a ninny that I thought: Thank God I'm getting married now, before I'm twenty-six and washed up.

Anyway, when Arnold the hamster died, Charlie took him to one of those cryogenic places and had him frozen. It wasn't at all expensive, because the body was so small, on top of which there wasn't any additional charge for storage because Charlie brought Arnold home in a nice Baggie with a rubber band around it and simply stuck him into the freezer. I could just see Cora Bigelow, the maid, taking Arnold out one Thursday thinking he was a newfangled freeze-dried potato treat in a boil bag; boy, would Charlie be in for a shock the next time he went to put an eensy-weensy bouquet of flowers next to Arnold's final resting place, directly to the right of the ice cube tray. I mean, what are you supposed to do with a first husband like that? I'll tell you what: divorce him. I'll tell you something else: when you divorce a first husband like that, you never look back. You never once think: God, I wish Charlie were here, he'd know how to handle this. Charlie never handled anything if he could help it. He just made a note of it in his Mark Cross datebook and erased it when the problem had cleared up.

I left Charlie after six years, although at least two of those years were spent beating a dead horse. There have always been many things you can do short of actually ending a bad marriage—buying a house, having an affair and having a baby are the most common, I suppose—but in the early 1970s there were at least two more. You could go into consciousness raising and spend an evening a week talking over cheese to seven other women whose marriages were equally unhappy. And you could sit down with your husband and thrash everything out in a wildly irrelevant fashion by drawing up a list of household duties and dividing them up all over again. This happened in thousands of households, with identical results: thousands of husbands agreed to clear the table. They cleared the table. They cleared the table and then looked around as if they deserved a medal. They cleared the table and then hoped they would never again be asked to do another thing. They cleared the table and hoped the whole thing would go away. And it did. The women's movement went away, and so, in many cases, did their wives. Their wives went out into the world, free at last, single again, and discovered the horrible truth: that they were sellers in a buyers' market, and that the major concrete achievement of the women's movement in the 1970s was the Dutch treat.

I left Charlie everything—the cooperative apartment, the house in the country, and Shirley, Mendel, Manny and Fletcher. I took my clothes and my kitchen equipment and two couches I had brought to the marriage. I asked Charlie for a coffee table, but he wouldn't give it to me. The moving man sat there reading the section on vaginal self-examination in my spare copy of *Our Bodies, Ourselves* while Charlie and I fought about furniture. I said we had three coffee tables; the least he could do was to give me one. He said I had both couches and where was he supposed to sit anyway. I said that I'd brought both couches to the marriage, but that all three coffee tables had been accumulated *during* the marriage and I ought to get *something* that had been accumulated during the marriage. He said I could have Mendel. I said Mendel was a washout, even for a hamster. He said he'd brought furniture to the marriage, too, but that I'd given it to my mother when she'd run off with the Mel who was God and it had never been seen again. I said the furniture we'd given to my mother was Swedish modern and revolting and we owed the Mel who was God a big favor for taking it off our hands. He said he would never give me the coffee table because he'd just realized I'd packed the carrot peeler along with my kitchen equipment and now he had no way to make lunch for Shirley and the boys. On his way out to buy another carrot peeler, he said he would never forgive me for what I'd said about Mendel. At the end of the move, the mover shook my hand solemnly and said, "I had five others this week just like this one. Yours wasn't so bad."

Of course, afterward Vera said I'd set it up so it would happen that way, set it up so that there would be no way Charlie could possibly give me the coffee table and I could therefore walk away from the marriage with the happy knowledge that Charlie was as stingy as I'd always said he was. "You picked him," Vera said, "because his neuroses meshed perfectly with yours." I love Vera, truly I do, but *doesn't anything happen to you that you don't intend*? "You picked him because you knew it wouldn't work out." "You picked him because his neuroses meshed perfectly with yours." "You picked him because you knew he'd deprive you the way your mother or your father did." That's what they're always telling you, one way or another, but the truth is that no matter whom you pick, it doesn't work out; the truth is that no matter whom you pick, your neuroses mesh perfectly and horribly; the truth is that no matter whom you pick, he deprives you the way your mother or your father did. "You picked the one person on earth you could have problems with." "You picked the one person on earth you shouldn't be involved with." There's nothing brilliant about that—that's life. Every time you turn around you get involved with the one person on earth you shouldn't get involved with. Robert Browning's shrink probably said it to *him*. "So, Robert, it's very interesting, no? Of all the women in London, you pick this hopeless invalid who has a crush on her father." Let's face it: *everyone* is the one person on earth you shouldn't get involved with.

And what is all this about *picking*, anyway? Who's picking? When I was in college, I had a list of what I wanted in a husband. A long list. I wanted a registered Democrat, a bridge player, a linguist with particular fluency in French, a subscriber to *The New Republic*, a tennis player. I wanted a man who wasn't bald, who wasn't fat, who wasn't covered with too much body hair. I wanted a man with long legs and a small ass and laugh wrinkles around the eyes. Then I grew up and settled for a low-grade lunatic who kept hamsters. At first I thought he was charming and eccentric. And then I didn't. Then I wanted to kill him. Every time he got on a plane, I would imagine the plane crash, and the funeral, and what I would wear to the funeral and flirting at the funeral, and how soon I could start dating after the funeral.

Is this inevitable, this moment when everything leads to irritation, when you become furious that he smokes, or that he coughs in the morning, or that he sheds crumbs, or that he exaggerates, or that he drives like a maniac, or that he says "Between you and I"? You fall in love with someone, and part of what

you love about him are the differences between you; and then you get married and the
differences start to drive you crazy. You fall in
love with someone and you say to yourself, oh,
well, I never really cared about politics,
bridge, French and tennis; and then you get
married and it starts to drive you crazy that
you're married to someone who doesn't even
know who's running for President. This is the
moment when any therapist will tell you that
your problem is fear of intimacy; that you're
connecting to your mother, or holding on to
your father. But it seems to me that what's
happening is far more basic; it seems to me
that it's just about impossible to live with
someone else.

And soon there's nothing left of the marriage but the moments of irritation, followed
by the apologies, followed by the moments of
irritation, followed by the apologies; and all
this is interspersed with decisions about
which chair goes in the den and whose dinner
party are we going to tonight. In the end,
what's left is a social arrangement. You are a
couple. You go places together. And then you
break up, and the moving man tells you yours
wasn't so bad. But it was. Even when you end
a marriage you want to end, it's awful.

I started out telling you all this because I
wanted you to understand why I so resisted
getting married again. It seemed to me that
the desire to get married—which, I regret to
say, I believe is fundamental and primal in

women—is followed almost immediately by an equally fundamental and primal urge, which is to be single again. But there was Mark. With his big brown eyes and his sweetheart roses. Forever and ever, he said. Forever and ever and ever, he said. *I'll be loving you always. . . . Not for just an hour, not for just a day, not for just a year, but always.*

For a long time, I didn't believe him. And then I believed him. I believed in change. I believed in metamorphosis. I believed in redemption. I believed in Mark. My marriage to him was as willful an act as I have ever committed; I married him against all the evidence. I married him believing that marriage doesn't work, that love dies, that passion fades, and in so doing I became the kind of romantic only a cynic is truly capable of being. I see all that now. At the time, though, I saw nothing of the sort. I honestly believed that Mark had learned his lesson. Unfortunately, the lesson he learned wasn't the one I had in mind: what he learned is that he could do anything, and in the end there was a chance I'd take him back.

VII

Your husband's here," Lucy Mae Hopkins said, as she opened the door to my father's apartment for me. Then she rolled her eyes. Lucy Mae Hopkins had given up men for Jesus forty years earlier, and she couldn't understand why anyone else wouldn't, given the choice. I walked into the living room. Mark was sitting on the couch, reading a book to Sam. He looked up and gave me a nod and went on reading. I sat down in a chair and noticed a blazer Mark had draped over the back of it. A new blazer. The man had broken my heart and then gone out and bought himself a new blazer! To make matters worse, it was a nice blazer. I fingered the material.

"Britches," said Mark. Britches is a store in Washington where Mark buys his clothes. The man had broken my heart and had then gone out and bought himself a new blazer and the first word out of his mouth was Britches!

Mark finished reading to Sam and sent him off to the kitchen for a cookie. He looked at me. "I'd like you to come back," he said.

I shook my head no, not because I was refusing but because I couldn't believe that that was all he had to say. Not a word about Thelma. Not a word about how he must have been crazy. Not a word about how he was sorry. Perhaps this is Mark's way of being understated, I thought. And then again, perhaps not. In fact, probably not. I kept on shaking my head. I couldn't stop shaking my head. "I love you," he said. He said it with the animation of a tree sloth. "I want you to come home," he said. "You belong at home."

"I'm not coming home if you're going to see her anymore," I said.

"I'm not going to see her anymore," he said.

There was a long silence. I kept expecting him to reach out for my hand, or touch my face. He didn't. Rachel, I said to myself, this will not do. You cannot go anywhere, much less home, with a man whose idea of an apology does not include even a hypocritical show of affection. Say no. Tell him to drop dead. Crack one of your father's atrocious lamps over his head. Go into the kitchen and invent the instant waffle. Anything.

"I know this is difficult for you," Mark said, "but it's difficult for me, too."

And then Mark started to cry. *Mark* started

to cry. I couldn't believe it. It seemed to me that if anyone was entitled to cry in this scene, it was going to be me; but the man had run off with my part. "I'm in a lot of pain," he said.

There has been a lot written in recent years about the fact that men don't cry enough. Crying is thought to be a desirable thing, a sign of a mature male sensibility, and it is generally believed that when little boys are taught that it is unmanly to cry, they grow up unable to deal with pain and grief and disappointment and feelings in general. I would like to say two things about this. The first is that I have always believed that crying is a highly overrated activity: women do entirely too much of it, and the last thing we ought to want is for it to become a universal excess. The second thing I want to say is this: beware of men who cry. It's true that men who cry are sensitive to and in touch with feelings, but the only feelings they tend to be sensitive to and in touch with are their own.

Not that I knew this at the time. If I had, I could have stayed in New York with my pathetic dreams of Detective Nolan and six kinds of smoked salmon. What I actually did, though, is that I looked at Mark, sitting there, a picture of misery, and I crumbled. I can't stand to see a man cry, that's the truth. I can't stand to see a woman cry either, but the only woman I ever really see crying to any extent is me, and even though you may think I do an awful lot of it for someone who can't stand to see it, the fact is that I cry much less now than I used to. When I was young, a rude salesman at the hardware store could make me cry.

"All right," I said to Mark. "I'll come home."

"Good," said Mark, and he stopped crying. "You can put the ring back on now," he said.

I shook my head no.

"For God's sake, Rachel," he said. "Put the ring back on."

"I gave it away," I said.

"You what?" he said.

"I gave it away."

"To whom?" he said.

"To a celebrity auction," I said.

"Is this a joke?" he said.

"Yes," I said, "and not a bad one, all things considered."

"Put the ring back on," he said.

"Only part of it was a joke," I said.

"Which part?" said Mark. Mark used to like the fact that I make jokes in adverse circumstances, but clearly the charm of that had begun to wear thin.

"The part about the celebrity auction was a joke," I said. "The part about giving it away wasn't."

"You gave the ring away," said Mark.

"Not of my own free will," I said.

"Someone took it away from you," said Mark.

"Yes," I said.

"Do you want me to guess who it was?" he said.

"My group was robbed," I said.

"That's funny," said Mark. He started to laugh. "By an outsider, or by someone in the group?"

"By an outsider," I said, "and it's not funny. He held a gun to my head."

"Just because you don't think it's funny doesn't mean I don't think it's funny," said Mark. "Maybe I can get a column out of it." He began to nod slowly, the way he does whenever he gets an idea for a column and it's just started ticking away. Mark writes three columns a week, and while most of them are about political life, just enough of them are about domestic life that I sometimes felt as if I were living with a cannibal; things barely finished happening before Mark was chewing away at them, trying to string them out, turn them upside down, blow them up into 850 words for tomorrow's newspaper. Sometimes, when he was really worried about what to write about next, he would sit at dinnertime, his eyes darting desperately around the room. Was there a column in the salt and pepper shakers? In the paper napkins? In the Cuisinart food processor? "Have you noticed how hard it is to peel a hard-boiled egg?" he'd say. "Yes," I'd say. "You think there's anything to it?" he'd say. Or: "Have you noticed that English muffins don't taste as good as they used to?" he'd say. "Yes," I'd say. "You think there's anything to it?" he'd say. I don't mean to sound innocent and passive about all this; I loved looking for things for Mark to write columns about. I brought home anecdotes about parking lot attendants and supermarket checkers for him to munch on. In fact, it occurs to me that one of the reasons I sometimes felt that nothing had happened to me since my marriage was that every time something *did* happen, Mark got a column out of it and in essence made it all seem as if it had happened to him. You should see the column he got out of Mr. Abbey's murder. *My* murder, my very own personal murder, and he ran off with it and turned it into an essay on homosexuals and urban crime and practically got us all killed by the Gay Rights League. He even raided Sam's life. Sam was barely two years old, and the column about the time he swallowed the nail polish remover had run in 109 papers and the one about his first dead guppy was about to be anthologized by the Oxford University Press. Someday Sam was going to grow up and sit down to write about his life and there wouldn't be anything left of it to write about.

"You can't get a column out of my group's robbery," I said.

"Why not?" said Mark.

"Because it happened to *me*," I said. "On top of which, it was really awful."

"I'm sorry," said Mark. "Did he hurt you?"

"He twisted my arm," I said.

"Show Daddy where," said Mark.

"Oh, shut up," I said. Then I smiled. I couldn't help it. And so did he.

"I'll buy you another ring," said Mark.

"We don't have the money for another ring," I said.

"That's true," said Mark. "We didn't even have the money to insure this one."

We sat and looked at each other for a moment.

"It's sort of fitting," I said.

"Meaning what?" said Mark.

"Meaning it was a symbol of how good things were, and now that things aren't, it's just as well it's not here to remind me."

"I hate it when you say things like that," said Mark.

"I know," I said. "Do you still love her?"

"I don't want to talk about it," he said.

"But you're not going to see her anymore," I said.

"I already said that," he said.

"And the two of you aren't going to see that Guatemalan frittata together anymore, either."

"Rachel."

"Just say yes or no."

"I told you I wasn't going to see Thelma anymore, so obviously we're not going to see Dr. Valdez together anymore, either."

"Good," I said.

"Thelma doesn't really believe in that stuff anyway," he said.

"I wouldn't either," I said, "if all I had to go on was that refried taco."

"Rachel."

"Yes."

"If we leave now we can make the last plane."

The last Eastern Airlines shuttle between New York and Washington leaves at nine o'clock at night. When Mark and I were single and he lived in Washington and I lived in New York, we could never have a serious fight late at night, because there was no way to slam out the door and go home. There was something I liked about the fact that our lives and temperaments were controlled by an airline schedule, but the truth is that there were many things I liked about the Eastern shuttle. Not the comfort, and not the courtesy of the flight attendants, both of which were negligible. But the things you were supposed to like. The fact that it tended to leave when it said it was going to and to get there on schedule an hour later. The fact that you didn't need a reservation and always got a seat. The fact that there was something so utterly no-nonsense about it, just like its passengers. No one ever seemed to be going from one end of the Eastern shuttle to the other for fun. No one ever seemed to be *traveling*. They were all simply going to meetings that were in offices that happened to be in another city. Everyone carried a briefcase. Everyone was dressed for success. Everyone was serious. Indeed, it seems to me that the Eastern shuttle was almost a perfect reflection of the Puritan tradition in its attempt to make a virtue out of suffering, abstinence and plainness; and it always seemed fitting that one Eastern shuttle flies New York to Boston, where the Puritan tradition began, and the other flies New York to Washington, where those produced by that tradition are rewarded with the power to force the rest of the country to heel to its values. I loved that it took such an austere conveyance to get me to Mark; there was something wonderfully romantic about it. I looked like everyone else on the shuttle, I dressed like everyone else, I carried the *New York Times* and the *Washington Post* and the *Wall Street Journal* like everyone else. But everyone else was on their way to work, and I was on my way to Mark.

Then, one day, Mark and I were on the Eastern shuttle and he asked me to marry him. This was when he was asking me to marry him a couple of times a week, but he had never asked me on the Eastern shuttle.

"This is your chance to say yes on the Eastern shuttle," he said.

"No," I said.

"This is your chance at a really bad metaphor," he said.

"No," I said.

"This is your last chance," he said. "I'll ask

you to marry me again and again, but I'll never again ask you on the Eastern shuttle."

So I said yes.

Our friends the Siegels gave us ten shares of Eastern Airlines stock for a wedding present. Ha ha. The fare on the shuttle went to fifty dollars. And to fifty-four dollars. And to fifty-eight dollars. Arthur Siegel said: "It's a good thing you two met before the fare went up, because no fuck is worth $116 round trip." Ha ha. I moved to Washington and Sam was born and Arthur said that the money I saved not taking the Eastern shuttle almost paid for the baby's diapers. Ha ha. Eastern shuttle jokes. Not particularly funny jokes, but what do you expect?

Anyway, just try flying the Eastern shuttle with a baby. Try flying any plane with a baby if you want a sense of what it must have been like to be a leper in the fourteenth century, but try the shuttle for the ultimate in shunning. All those men in suits, looking at you as if your baby is going to throw up over their speech drafts; all those men in suits who used to look at me with respect when I pulled out my American Express gold card, now barely able to conceal their contempt for me and my portable Wet Ones.

And just try flying the Eastern shuttle with a baby *and* with a husband who is barely speaking to you. Mark deserted me the minute we got to the terminal at La Guardia and went off to buy magazines and newspapers and to call the office to make sure something important hadn't happened while he was off in New York on a trivial personal errand. I got on line for the plane. Sam was cranky and tired, and I was holding him and the duffel bag and the shopping bag full of Pampers and trying to write out my boarding pass with a pencil stub and my glasses fell off my nose and when I leaned over to pick them up, a stack pack of Ritz crackers fell out of my pocket onto the floor. The man next to me in line picked them up and asked me if he could help. I almost cried; I wanted to cry, but I was afraid crying would make my glasses fall off my nose again. He was a dark-skinned man with a rather thrilling foreign accent I couldn't place. Gratefully I handed him the shopping bag, and he carried the duffel bag to the baggage conveyor belt. When he came back, he smiled, and I noticed he had three subcutaneous cysts on his face—those little lumps that save Robert Redford from being too handsome. I wondered if he'd consider having his subcutaneous cysts removed if we got married. I wondered if I could live with someone with a foreign accent. I wondered where he was from, and how his family would feel about his marrying a Jew. I wondered if wherever he was from was the kind of place where they refer to Jewish women as Jewesses.

"Where are you from?" I said.

"From?" he said.

"What country are you from?" I said.

"My cauntry," he said with a smile, "ees bery beautiful."

I nodded. He nodded. I nodded. He nodded. So much for marrying foreigners, I thought. So much for my vow not to have marital fantasies about strangers.

I took an aisle seat on the plane, put Sam in the middle, and saved the window for Mark. He turned up a few minutes later and handed me the early edition of the *Daily News*. There was Vanessa, on page one, coming out of the police precinct; she looked wonderful. Inside was a riveting story about the glamorous group and the robbery. The story identified me as a "cookbook author," which always irritates me a little bit since they aren't merely cookbooks, but at least it didn't say that I was a distraught, rejected, pregnant cookbook author whose husband was in love with a giantess. According to the article, Sidney and Dan not only discovered each other's last names at the police precinct but also discovered that they were distant cousins. I wasn't sure what the readers of the *Daily News* were going to make of that detail, but I was positive my group would waste hours discussing its possible relevance. In fact, it seemed to me it might make sense to disband the group entirely, since we were bound to be spending so much time in the next year talking about the robbery and its effect that we would never again have time to discuss anyone's actual life. I wondered whether Mark had read the story, but I knew that if I asked him what he thought of it he would simply use it as yet another occasion to insult my adventures in psychoanalysis in order to punish me for insulting his. I looked over at him. He was immersed in *Casa Vogue*. It was as if he were pretending he wasn't with me, that I was just some hopeless woman who didn't even bother to space her pregnancies, much less respond properly to sitting in the same row with important Washington journalists who are trying to concentrate on home-decorating tips. And I'll tell you the capper. The stewardess came down the aisle to collect the fares. Now, Mark and I always split things up. I paid my way; I always paid my way. We both earned money, and the money we earned went to pay for what we did. But wouldn't you think that on this night of all nights he ought to have put my shuttle fare on his credit card? Well, he didn't.

I looked at him and was about to say something, when Meg Roberts poked her head over the back of the seat in front of us.

"I thought I was going to see you at Betty's the other night," she said.

"Fare, please," said the stewardess.

I fished in my bag for my credit card and handed it to her.

"At Betty's?" I said.

"At her birthday party," Meg said.

"Omigod," I said. I looked at Mark. He

shook his head; he had forgotten, too. I was off in New York crying my eyes out, and he was in Washington fucking his brains out, and we had both forgotten Betty's thirty-ninth birthday party. The only way Betty would ever forgive me would be for me to tell her why, and if I told her why she'd tell everyone in Washington, and then everyone in town would know something about our marriage that I didn't want them to know. I know all about Meg Roberts' marriage, for example, because Meg confides in her friend Ann, who confides in Betty, who confides in me. What I know is that Meg Roberts sleeps with presidential candidates, and her husband sleeps with presidential candidates' press secretaries' secretaries. They seem very happy.

"How was the party?" said Mark.

"Wonderful," said Meg, and popped back down.

Actually, there is no possible way a seated dinner party in Washington can ever be wonderful. After only half an hour of drinks, you are seated, seated forever, trapped between two immensely powerful men who think it's your function as their dinner partner to draw them out. You draw them out. You ask them about the Salt talks. You ask them about the firearms lobby. You ask them about their constituencies. You ask them about the next election. Dinner ends and everyone goes home. It always amazes me that women like Meg Roberts ever manage to get anything sexual going in Washington, although obviously she knows something about drawing men out that I don't.

Sam threw up on Mark's new blazer.

"Shit," said Mark.

"I'm sorry," I said. Sam started to cry. There was a kind of odd murmur in the seats around us, as the smell began to penetrate to the adjoining rows. At any moment the murmur would probably build to a hiss, and then to a chorus of boos, and ultimately Sam and I would be stoned to death with Bic pens.

"What am I apologizing for?" I said. "It's not my fault."

"I know it's not," said Mark. "I'm sorry."

"It's not your fault either," I said.

"This whole thing is my fault," he said.

"If you really believed that, you would have paid my shuttle fare," I said.

I picked up Sam and stood up to go to the bathroom with him. Mark began to wipe off his blazer with his handkerchief.

"You bought that blazer with Thelma Rice, didn't you?" I said, and started for the back. I didn't even have to hear the answer. Mark's impulse to fall in love is always accompanied by his impulse to purchase clothes with the loved one looking on. Sometimes it seemed to me that I had spent half my marriage in the men's department watching small white-haired tailors on their knees making chalk marks on Mark's trouser cuffs.

I went back to the bathroom and laid Sam

on the top of the toilet seat to change his clothes. Toilet seats in airplane bathrooms are not even big enough to change baby piglets on. Sam's head kept flopping off the cliff sides of the toilet seat as I changed his overalls and T-shirt and diaper. When I finished, I checked out the mirror to see if I looked older, or sadder, or wiser. I didn't; I just looked tired. Well, I was going home. I was going home with my husband. I loved my husband. The city of New York was a wonderful place, but it seemed terribly unimportant next to my marriage. So much for sorrel soup. I had never thought my marriage could survive an infidelity, but it would. It had been unrealistic of me to expect that the situation would never come up. They say all marriages go through something like this. I became dizzy as the clichés raced through my head. I put Sam on the bathroom floor and threw up. In the main cabin, the pilot was announcing our descent to the Washington area. Yes indeed, I thought. I wiped myself off and went back to my seat.

VIII

I see that I haven't managed to work in any recipes for a while. It's hard to work in recipes when you're moving the plot forward. Not that this book has an enormous amount of plot, but it has more plot than I've ever dealt with before. My other books just meandered from one person to the next, whereas this one has a story with a beginning and an end. That's one of the things that makes it different from most of what has happened to me in my life: I know when it began and when it ended. When my first marriage collapsed, I made a lot of notes about the hamsters and the fight over the coffee table, but I could never be sure whether the end of my marriage to Charlie was the beginning of a story or the end of one. But the story I'm telling here began the day I discovered the affair between Mark and Thelma, and it ended exactly six weeks later. It has a happy ending, but that's because I insist on happy endings; I would insist on happy beginnings, too, but that's not necessary because all beginnings are intrinsically happy, in my opinion. What about middles, you may ask. Middles are a problem. Middles are perhaps the major problem of contemporary life.

In any case, all I meant to say was that because this book tells a story, there aren't as many recipes in it as there are in my other books, so if you bought it because you thought there were going to be lots of recipes in every chapter, I'm sorry.

On the other hand, I've gotten to the point in the story where I return to Washington, and that brings me to the Siegels, finally to the Siegels; and therefore it brings me to the linguine alla cecca recipe. The four of us went to Italy a few years ago, and Julie Siegel and I managed to wangle the recipe from the proprietor of a restaurant in Rome. We also spent quite a lot of time after that trip working in pesto, because we went to Italy in 1977, and in 1977 everyone was eating pesto. As Arthur Siegel said one day: "Pesto is the quiche of the seventies." Arthur had a way of saying things like that—of summing up the situation so perfectly that you never wanted another spoonful of pesto again—and whenever he said something like that, Mark always ran off with it and turned it into a column. Arthur used to complain bitterly about having his best remarks stolen, but the truth is he rather liked it; he was a running character in Mark's columns, and he enjoyed a certain notoriety at Georgetown Law School, where he taught criminal law while waiting for the Kennedys to return to power. As for the linguine alla cecca, it's a hot pasta with a cold tomato and basil sauce, and it's so light and delicate that it's almost like eating a salad. It has to be made in the summer, when tomatoes are fresh. Drop 5 large tomatoes into boiling water for one full minute. Peel and seed and chop. Put into a large bowl with ½ cup olive oil, a garlic clove sliced in two, 1 cup chopped fresh basil leaves, salt and hot red pepper flakes. Let sit for a couple of hours, then remove the garlic. Boil one pound of linguine, drain and toss with the cold tomato mixture. Serve immediately.

Arthur and Julie and Mark and Rachel. The Siegels and the Feldmans. It's not just that we were best friends—we dated each other. We went steady. That's one of the things that happens when you become a couple: you date other couples. We saw each other every Saturday night and every Sunday night, and we had a standing engagement for New Year's Eve. Our marriages were tied together. We went to Italy, we went to Ireland, we went to Williamsburg, we went to Montreal, we went to St. Martin, and Mark drove and I navigated and Julie suggested wrong turns and Arthur fell asleep. Then, when we got to wherever we were going, Mark wanted to eat and I wanted to see the market and Julie wanted to go to the museum and Arthur wanted to take a crap. We had flat tires together and we ran out of gas together; in some fundamental sense, we were always on the road, merrily on our way to nowhere in particular. Two of us liked dark meat and two of us liked light meat and together we made a chicken.

I suppose that I honestly believed that if I couldn't save our marriage, the Siegels could. Which is why I called them from New York the night I discovered Mark's affair. They were shocked. They were astonished. There was consternation in every syllable they uttered. All of this was a relief to me—suppose they'd known! Suppose they'd known and hadn't told me! Suppose they'd known and told me!

"With Thelma Rice?" Julie said on the phone. "Omigod."

"Julie, what am I going to do?" I said.

"Pick up the phone, Arthur," said Julie. "It's Rachel."

"Hello," said Arthur.

"I'm sorry to call so late," I said.

"That's okay," said Arthur. "Obviously you've finally figured out who Thelma Rice is having the affair with and you're calling to tell us, and I appreciate it even if it is one in the morning."

"It's Mark," I said.

"Did something happen to Mark?" said Arthur. "Jesus Christ, Rachel. What is it?"

"Arthur," said Julie, "Thelma Rice is having the affair with Mark."

"He says he's in love with her," I said.

"He told you this?" said Arthur.

"Yes," I said.

"Why did he tell you this?" said Arthur.

"I found a book she'd given him with an inscription in it, and when I confronted him, he said he was in love with her."

"He said he was in love with her or he said he was fucking her?" said Arthur.

"He said he was in love with her but he said he wasn't fucking her," I said.

"Where are you?" said Julie.

"In New York," I said. "At my father's."

"Where's Sam?" said Julie.

"With me," I said.

"Does he know what's happening?" said Arthur.

"I don't think so," I said. "I've been crying for eight hours now, and he hasn't even noticed."

"I know," said Julie. "When Alexandra was two I cried for eight *months* and she never noticed."

"Does Mark know you're there?" said Arthur.

"I don't know," I said.

"That fuckhead," said Arthur. "He's gone crazy."

"That's what I said to him," I said. "But he denied it."

"Of course he denied it," said Arthur. "That's the truest sign of insanity—insane people are always sure they're just fine. It's only the sane people who are willing to admit they're crazy."

"Did you know about this, Arthur?" said Julie.

"Of course I didn't know about it," said Arthur. "How could you think I would know about it and not tell you?"

"I told him he had to stop seeing her," I said.

"And what did he say?" said Arthur.

"He said he wouldn't. And he said I should stay with him anyway and have the baby. He said, 'I am in love with Thelma Rice. I still have feelings about you, of course, and we are going to have another baby, so I suggest we just get from day to day.'"

"Oh, shit," said Julie.

"Listen, Rachel, sit tight," said Arthur. "I'm going to talk to him."

Arthur and Julie will go over there and beat some sense into Mark, I thought when I hung up the phone. Arthur and Julie will glare at him until he withers under the moral opprobrium of their gaze. Arthur and Julie will take the power of our friendship and club him into submission. This was not exactly the romantic scenario I had had in mind—I would have preferred Mark to have a more voluntary kind

of blinding vision—but it would have to do.
After all, Mark might be willing to give me
up, and my vinaigrette, but he would never
give up the four of us. And Thelma would
never fit in. For one thing, she was too tall.
Arthur and Julie and Mark and I were all
approximately the same size, which is one
reason we traveled so well together. It's hard
to walk in lockstep with people a lot taller
than you are, because they take longer strides,
and you always feel like a little puppy scamp-
ering to keep up. For another thing, Thelma
Rice really didn't care about food—that was
clear from her gluey puddings—while the four
of us had a friendship that was a shrine to
food. We had driven miles to find the world's
creamiest cheesecake and the world's largest
pistachio nut and the world's sweetest corn on
the cob. We had spent hours in blind taste
testings of kosher hot dogs and double chocolate chip ice cream. When Julie went home to
Fort Worth, she flew back with spare ribs from
Angelo's Beef Bar-B-Q, and when I went to
New York, I flew back with smoked butterfish
from Russ and Daughters. Once, in New Or-
leans, we all went to Mosca's for dinner, and
we ate marinated crab, baked oysters, barbecued shrimp, spaghetti bordelaise, chicken
with garlic, sausage with potatoes, and on the
way back to town, a dozen oysters each at the
Acme and beignets and coffee with chicory on
the wharf. Then Arthur said, "Let's go to

Chez Helene for the bread pudding," and we did, and we each had two. The owner of Chez Helene gave us the recipe when we left, and I'm going to throw it in because it's the best bread pudding I've ever eaten. It tastes like caramelized mush. Cream 2 cups sugar with 2 sticks butter. Add six beaten eggs, then add 2½ cups milk, one 13–ounce can evaporated milk, 2 tablespoons nutmeg, 2 tablespoons vanilla, a loaf of wet bread in chunks and pieces (any bread will do, the worse the better) and 1 cup raisins. Stir to mix. Pour into a deep greased casserole and bake at 350° for 2 hours, stirring after the first hour. Serve warm with hard sauce.

For the most part, Arthur Siegel is remarkably content. Once when we played Do You Have Any Regrets, the only thing he could come up with was that we hadn't ordered some fried onion rings at Chez Helene along with the bread pudding. When we played What Do You Wish You Were Named, I wanted to be named Veronica because it's luscious and I'm not, Julie wanted to be named Anthea because it's thin and she's not, Mark wanted to be named Sasha because it's dashing and he's not, and Arthur thought it over and said it seemed to him his name suited him just fine. It does. Arthur is chunky but solid, as an Arthur should be, and he has a red handlebar mustache that almost compensates for the fact that he is almost completely bald. I'll tell you how sensible Arthur is: he doesn't even mind being bald.

Arthur and Mark had grown up together in Brooklyn. They went to Columbia, and then Mark went to journalism school there and Arthur went off to law school at Yale. They both ended up in Washington. Julie was a legislative assistant on Capitol Hill when Arthur met her. She has curly blond hair and goo-goo-googly eyes and big pearly teeth like the girl in the Coca-Cola ad, and every so often Arthur stares across the room at her as if he cannot believe she's his. All of this is mystifying to Julie, who believes she's just a fairly average plump girl from Texas who snagged a nice Jewish husband solely due to what she calls shiksa madness.

The Siegels got married and moved into a two-bedroom apartment on Connecticut Avenue, and Mark would bring his girl friends to breakfast on Sundays. The first Jewish Kimberly passed through their lives. Then more girl friends. Then Mark turned up with me, and suddenly there we were, the four of us. Together. We would sit around, doing nothing, nothing at all, lazy Sundays with clouds in the coffee and papers all over the living room and dusty Sunday light coming through the color-coordinated Levolor blinds. Arthur would say that the trouble with Washington was that there wasn't a decent delicatessen. Julie would say that the trouble with Washington was that there weren't any late movies on television. I would say that the trouble with Washington was that it was so goyish. Mark would say that the trouble with Washington was that too many people there spent too much time figuring out what the trouble with it was. We would all say these things as if we had never said them before, and argue over them as if we had never argued over them before. Then we would all decide whether we wanted to be buried or cremated. Then we would move on to the important matters. Should they paint their living room peach? Should they strip down their dining table? Should they buy a videotape recorder? Should they re-cover the couch?

"I don't see what was wrong with it before," said Arthur after they re-covered the couch.

"Nothing was wrong with it before," said Julie.

"What color is this anyway?" said Arthur.

"Taupe," said Julie.

Arthur shook his head. "I've always been terrible at colors," he said. "It comes from having grown up with the single-row box of crayons instead of the big box. If I'd had the big box I would now know taupe and cerise and ecru. Instead, all I know is burnt sienna. And what good does it do me? Never once have I heard anything described as burnt sienna. Never once have I heard anyone say, 'Follow that burnt sienna car.'"

"I think there's a column in this," said Mark.

"Goddammit, Feldman," said Arthur.

"You can have it if you want it," said Mark.

"What do you mean, I can have it if I want it?" said Arthur. "It's *mine*. *I'm* the one who gets to say, 'You can have it if you want it.' Not you."

"What are you going to do with it?" said Mark. "Write it up for the *Yale Law Review*?"

"He doesn't have to do *anything* with it," I said. "He can simply add it to his repertoire."

"Thanks, Rachel," said Arthur. He looked at Mark. "Don't break up with her, okay?" he said. "Promise me you won't."

"Jesus Christ," said Mark. "You'd think *you* were going with her."

"We are," said Arthur. "The two of us are going with the two of you."

"You used to like me when I was unattached," said Mark.

"Not as much as I like you as a couple," said Arthur, and he gave Mark a playful punch on the arm.

"You're punching me because you want me to think you're kidding, but you're not," said Mark.

"You'll never know, will you?" said Arthur. "The truth is, I wish you two would get married."

"Arthur, for God's sake," said Julie.

"I can't help it," said Arthur. "I like being married. I want everyone I care about to be married. That's the kind of guy I am. Warm. Generous. Expansive. Charming."

"You just want everyone to be in the same pot you're in," said Mark.

"I like the pot I'm in," said Arthur. "I like how it goes along. What's for dinner and which movie should we see and where are my socks."

"Where are your socks?" said Mark. "Where are my socks? Where are all the missing socks?"

"They're in heaven," said Arthur. "You die, you go to heaven, and they bring you a big box, and it's got all your lost socks in it, and your mufflers and your gloves, and you get to spend eternity sorting them all out."

"I think there's a column in this," said Mark.

"Goddammit, Feldman," said Arthur.

Mark and I got married. You should have seen Arthur at the wedding. He stood with his head cocked at a jaunty angle, winking wildly and uncontrollably at the judge. He had done it. He had talked Mark into it. By the simple example of his own contentment, he had persuaded his best friend to give up bachelorhood. At the end of the ceremony, he whipped a glass from his pocket and placed it on the ground, and when Mark smashed it into the judge's Oriental rug, Arthur whooped around the room and danced the kazatsky. Three months later, I was walking up Connecticut Avenue, through the park at Dupont Circle, and there were Arthur and an unidentified female in a mad clinch on the park bench.

"I saw Arthur this afternoon," I said when I got home. "Kissing a . . ." I gestured absently with my hand and shook my head.

"Woman," said Mark.

"How long have you known about it?" I said.

"I don't know anything about it," said Mark. "I was just finishing the sentence. With Arthur, he's kissing a woman or a bagel. I took a guess." He looked at me. "Who was she?"

"I don't know."

"What did she look like?"

"Thin. Pretty. Big tits. Your basic nightmare."

We looked at each other.

"Should we do anything?" I said.

"He's my friend," said Mark. "We don't meddle in each other's lives."

"Of course we do," I said, "we meddle constantly. That's what true friendship is about."

"What did you have in mind?" said Mark.

"I don't know," I said.

"Maybe it's just a fling," said Mark. "He's almost forty, he probably feels nothing's happening to him—"

"It's just a passage," I said angrily.

"Yeah," said Mark.

"Shit," I said.

"Look, I hated the book as much as you did," said Mark.

"I know," I said. "I just feel betrayed. Never

mind Julie—he's cheating on us, you know what I mean?"

"I know what you mean," said Mark.

"One of the things I love about you is that you know what I mean even when I don't," I said.

"Actually, I don't," said Mark. "I just say I do."

"Maybe it's not serious," I said.

"Maybe it's just a fuck," said Mark.

"Yeah," I said.

"And I'm a ballerina," said Mark.

Two nights later, Arthur rang the bell in the middle of the night and announced that he was in love.

"A stewardess?" said Mark.

"A flight attendant," said Arthur.

"You must really be in love," said Mark.

"I am," said Arthur.

"Is this a midlife crisis or something?" said Mark.

"Don't reduce my life to some dime-store philosophy so it's easier for you to handle," said Arthur. "For twenty years I've watched you fuck around and fuck up and cheat on this one and cheat on that one. Did I ever judge you? Did I ever purse my lips? Did I ever say tch tch tch? Did you ever hear those words from me?"

"Tch tch tch?" said Mark. "Those words? I never heard those words because your tongue was so busy hanging out of your mouth you couldn't get them out. Listen to me. You're married. You've been married eight years. You've got a kid. Don't throw it away for a fuck."

"I suppose you're going to tell me things are going to be the same in bed with you and Rachel after eight years," said Arthur.

"No," said Mark, "but it'll still be good."

"It just won't be as often," said Arthur. "Instead of a couple of times a week it'll be a couple of times a year."

"I'll be almost fifty in ten years," said Mark.

"You know how old you have to be before you stop wanting to fuck strangers?" said Arthur. "Dead, that's how old. It doesn't stop. It doesn't go away. You put all this energy into suppressing it and telling yourself it's worth it because of what you get in exchange, and then one day someone brushes up against you and you're fourteen years old again and all you want to do is go to a drive-in movie and fuck her brains out in the back seat. But you don't do it because you're not going to be that kind of person, so you go home, and there's your wife, and she wears socks to bed."

"Socks again," said Mark.

On and on they went. It was late. Two in the morning. Three in the morning. We sat around the kitchen table in the yellow glow of the high-crime lights on the street, and I listened to Mark. Marriage was a trust, he said. Betray that trust and you have nothing, he said. I felt so smug. My husband the convert. My husband the true believer. My husband the husband. See a marriage counselor, he said. Do something.

And they did. The Siegels went to see a very nice marriage counselor named Gwendolyn. Gwendolyn left her husband three months later, but the Siegels survived. The four of us resumed normal activities. We went to Ohio for the shoofly pie and we went to Virginia for the ham. We were able to discuss other friends' marital difficulties without Julie's looking hurt and Arthur's looking guilty. Last summer they came to visit us in West Virginia, and Julie and I spent a week perfecting the peach pie. We made ordinary peach pie, and deep-dish peach pie, and blueberry and peach pie, but here is the best peach pie we made: Put 1¼ cups flour, ½ teaspoon salt, ½ cup butter and 2 tablespoons sour cream into a Cuisinart and blend until they form a ball. Pat out into a buttered pie tin, and bake 10 minutes at 425°. Beat 3 egg yolks slightly and combine with 1 cup sugar, 2 tablespoons flour and ⅓ cup sour cream. Pour over 3 peeled, sliced peaches arranged in the crust. Cover with foil. Reduce the oven to 350° and bake 35 minutes. Remove the foil and bake 10 minutes more, or until the filling is set.

I keep thinking about that week in West Virginia. It was a perfect week. We swam in the river and barbecued ribs and made Bellinis with crushed peaches and cheap champagne. We lay out on the lawn, the sunlight dappling through the copper beech, and Alexandra got her kite into the air and Sam applauded madly and scampered behind her, screaming with joy. Is it hot enough for you, we said, and the water isn't cold once you get in. We methodically rubbed sun block onto the arms of our children and poured another pitcherful into our glasses. So we were grownups. So what? Arthur lifted his glass. "I love you," he said. "I love us." The phone rang. Mark ran to get it and then called me into the house. We stood with the phone between us and listened to the lady in the hospital say that she had the results of the amniocentesis. The baby was normal. It was a boy. We ran back to the Siegels and drank to the baby. "You're going to have a brother," we told Sam. He started to cry. "Nathaniel," I said. "Can you say Nathaniel?" "No," said Sam. "Tummy hurts." Mark took him then, and walked him down to the river. They found a frog. Sam held it cupped in his hands, and giggled. I remember thinking: Lucky me, lucky us, lucky Sam, lucky Nathaniel. *What's wrong with this picture?*

IX

Arthur and Julie lived just a few blocks from our house. The morning after Mark and I got back to Washington, I slid out of bed and went over to see them. Arthur opened the door and gave me the kind of look you give some-one who's just had a death in the family and hugged me in a long, speechless, what-can-I-say sort of way.

"How are you?" he said.

"I'm back," I said. "How am I?"

"You're back," he said.

"Mark came to New York yesterday," I said. "He said he would stop seeing Thelma, so I came back."

Arthur nodded.

"What do you think?" I said.

"I don't know," said Arthur.

Julie came out from the bedroom. She put her arms around me and patted me quite a lot, and I cried on the shoulder of her terry-cloth bathrobe.

"Did you see him?" I said.

They nodded.

"I even saw her for a few minutes," said Arthur.

"Look," I said, "I'm putting you in an awkward position here."

"No, no," said Julie.

"What did he say?" I said.

"It doesn't matter," said Arthur.

"Why doesn't it matter?" I said.

"Because he's crazy," said Arthur.

We went into the kitchen and sat down with some of Arthur's fetishistically brewed coffee. Arthur makes coffee by putting eggshells and cinnamon sticks and an old nylon stocking into the coffeepot. His coffee tastes like a very spicy old foot.

"The week you came to West Virginia two months ago," I said.

"What about it?" said Arthur.

"Did we have a good time that week?"

"Terrific," said Julie.

"Did Mark and I seem happy?"

"Yes," said Julie.

"I was wondering about it," I said, "because Mark told me that our marriage had been terrible for a long time, and now I can't remember whether or not it was."

"He told us that, too," said Arthur.

"What else did he tell you?" I said.

"He said you were mean to him," said Arthur.

"I probably am," I said.

"Don't be ridiculous," said Julie.

"I am," I said. "All summer long I was snapping at him because he was never there."

"Of course you were snapping at him," said Julie. "He was having an affair."

"But I didn't know," I said.

"You must have known," said Arthur. "I knew."

"I thought you said you didn't know," said Julie.

"I didn't know about Thelma," said Arthur, "and I didn't know for sure, but I thought he was up to something. All those trips to the dentist."

"What was the matter with me?" I said. "If you could see it, why couldn't I?"

"Stop beating up on yourself," said Julie. "You trusted him. You have to trust someone you're married to, otherwise you'd spend your entire life going through the phone bills and American Express receipts."

"It's going to be all right," said Arthur.

"You're only saying that because you have to leave to teach a class and it's a good exit line," I said.

"I'm saying it because I have to leave and teach a class," said Arthur, "but it's true. He'll come to his senses. Jesus Christ, Rachel. Sam's still a baby and you're pregnant."

Arthur kissed us both goodbye and went out the door. Julie waited until she was sure he'd taken the elevator.

"I didn't know Mark was having an affair," said Julie. "I want you to know that. I don't know what I would have done if I'd known, but I didn't know."

"I know," I said. "What should I do, Julie?"

"Go home. Go on working. Take care of Sam. Have the baby. Wait the thing out. Eventually he'll get tired of her. Eventually she'll turn into as big a nag as he thinks you are. Eventually he'll get just as bored in bed with her as he is with you. And when that happens, he'll decide that it's less trouble to stay with you."

"But Mark isn't going to see Thelma anymore," I said. "So how is he going to get tired of her?"

"He will," said Julie.

"He will what?" I said.

"He'll see her again, and he'll get tired of her."

"And I'm supposed to sit there like a lox in the meantime?"

"Yes," said Julie. "If you want to stay married."

"That's a terrible thing to say," I said.

"I know," said Julie, "but it works. I did it. Sometimes I don't know why I did it, because it's so horrible and painful and humiliating, waiting the damned thing out. Sometimes I think I'd have been better off if I'd just left."

"Aren't you glad you're still with Arthur?"

"Oh, sure," said Julie.

"Then what is it?"

"I don't know," said Julie. "Sometimes the idea of being single interests me. For example, I woke up this morning and realized I'm never going to have bondage. It's just never going to come up with me and Arthur. I don't want to have it particularly, but it's never going to come up."

"I've never done it either," I said, "though I guess if I wanted to I could always ask."

"Arthur would just laugh at me," said Julie.

"Although I'm not sure what Mark would tie me to," I said, "since we don't have a headboard. You pretty much need a headboard, don't you think?"

"I don't know," said Julie. "That's the whole point."

"I guess you could always check into a hotel," I said. "Hotel beds have headboards."

"You could call room service for the rope," said Julie.

"It's really bad, isn't it?" I said.

"It's always bad when it happens," said Julie. "And then it gets better. You'll see. In a while, you'll be able to spend entire fifteen-minute periods without thinking about what they did together."

"And in the meantime," I said, "I can think about all the things in my future if it doesn't work out."

"What besides bondage?" said Julie.

"Amyl nitrates," I said. "Threesomes. Japanese movies. Roller disco. Thai food."

"I thought you hated Thai food," said Julie.

"I do," I said, "and if my marriage breaks up, I'll never have to have it again. It may be worth it."

Julie looked at me. "I think something happens to them," she said.

"You mean men," I said.

"I'm not saying they're worse," said Julie. "I'm saying they're different."

"You are too saying they're worse," I said.

"I know," said Julie.

"So what do we do?" I said.

"We hang on," she said, "and if it doesn't work, we try again with the next one."

When I got home, Mark was out in his office writing a jolly column about the Eastern shuttle. I walked into the kitchen and found Sam with Juanita, the maid. She was teaching him to say "Lie down with dogs, get up with fleas" in Spanish, which in some ways is the motto for Juanita's life. Juanita had lain down for twelve years with her husband, Hernando, and when he finally crawled out of her life, taking her Sears, Roebuck charge card with him, he left behind a rash of bad debts and old girl friends and faulty automobile parts that seemed destined to dominate Juanita's life forever. At least once a week she would turn up late for work, and explain through sobs that the Sears credit department was about to seize a stereo component she knew nothing about, or that her husband had stolen the spare tire from her car trunk, or that someone named Theresa had turned up at the front door asking for Hernando's stopwatch. "I tol' her he takes two minutes, drunk or sober," said Juanita. "What she need to time it for?" Juanita was a very brave woman, really—she was single-handedly supporting her three children—and I always tried very hard to love her, but she made it difficult because she was so disaster-prone. One morning, for example, on her way to work, she was stuck in a traffic jam on the Beltway, and when she got out of her car to see what was holding things up, in that split second, someone crept in through the passenger door of her car and stole her purse. Another time, she was standing in line in the Georgetown Safeway when a woman in front of her collapsed, and after Juanita revived her with mouth-to-mouth resuscitation, the woman tried to have her arrested for making improper advances.

Juanita looked up from Sam when I came in and burst into tears.

"Juanita," I said, "I'm not up for this. Whatever it is, I'm not up for it."

"Oh, Missee Felman, I feel so bad for ju," said Juanita. Even Juanita knew about it! The day after I'd left for New York she'd turned up to discover Mark and Thelma having a heart-to-heart talk on the living room couch.

"I know that lady," said Juanita. "She no good."

"I know," I said.

"*I* know," said Juanita. "I work for her ten years ago."

"What's wrong with her?" I said.

"She very messy," said Juanita.

Juanita gave me a big hug, which was awkward since she was only about four feet six inches tall, and a hug from her felt like the Heimlich maneuver. Then she pulled back and managed a huge smile that was meant to cheer me up—but instead revealed her mouthful of gold teeth, which only served to remind me of the time I had spent two days on the telephone with her dentist, negotiating a long-term payment for Hernando's root canal work.

"Everything be okay," she said. "You see."

I went up to the little room on the third floor that I used for an office. In the typewriter was an article I'd been writing about potatoes. I took it out of the typewriter and put in a fresh sheet of paper. I must write all this down, I thought. Someday I may write something that's not a cookbook, and this will all be grist for it. But I couldn't. To write it down was to give it permanence, to admit that something real had happened. I walked around the room trying to pretend that nothing had happened. I thought about potatoes. The first time I made dinner for Mark I made potatoes. The first time I made dinner for just about anyone I ever cared for I made potatoes. Very very crisp potatoes. I must make some potatoes tonight, I thought; mashed potatoes. Nothing like mashed potatoes when you're feeling blue. I could hear Mark's typewriter from the office over the garage; I kept hoping he would leave, go out for more socks, so I could dash into his sanctuary and go through the phone bills and the American Express receipts, but he was still there, tapping away. Maybe *he's* making notes for a novel, I thought. Worse, maybe he's making notes for a *column*. That would really do it. There would be my entire marital disaster, reduced to an 850-word column in 109 newspapers. I knew just how he'd write it, too. He'd write it in that dumb Hemingway style he always reserved for his slice-of-life columns. *The old man had told him it would happen. The old man had said to him, Sasha, it will happen someday. You will be on the river. You will be going downstream. You will hit a log.*

The phone rang.

I picked it up.

"Rachel, it's Betty."

"Oh, God," I said. "I'm so sorry."

"I know, I know," said Betty.

"You know?" I said.

"It must have been awful," said Betty.

"How do you know?" I said.

"It's in the paper," said Betty.

"In the paper?" I said.

"Why didn't you tell me that Vanessa Melhado was in your group?" said Betty.

"The robbery's in the paper?" I said.

"In the Style section," said Betty.

"We're not allowed to tell anyone who's in the group," I said.

"What's she like?"

"We're not allowed to tell that either," I said. "Listen, I feel terrible about missing your party."

"I understand," said Betty. "I knew something awful must have happened to you if you weren't there, and now I see that it did."

"Yes," I said. "It was awful."

"Anyway, it doesn't matter," said Betty, "because I found out who Thelma Rice is having the affair with."

"Who?" I said.

"You're not going to like it," said Betty.

"Who is it?" I said.

"Arthur," said Betty.

"Arthur Siegel?" I said.

"Yes," said Betty. "They were having drinks in the Washington Hilton yesterday afternoon. Nobody has drinks in the Washington Hilton unless something secret's going on."

"Arthur isn't having an affair with Thelma Rice," I said. "Nobody is having an affair with Thelma Rice."

"How do you know?" said Betty.

"I just know," I said.

"Tell me," said Betty.

"Okay," I said, "but you can't tell this to anyone."

"I promise," said Betty.

"I saw Thelma at the gynecologist's, and that's when I found out."

"What?" said Betty.

"She has this horrible infection," I said. "You don't even want to know about it."

"Oh, God," said Betty.

"She made me promise not to tell anyone," I said, "but she almost didn't have to because it's so disgusting I almost couldn't. I'm only telling you because I want you to know it's not true about her and Arthur."

"Then why was she having a drink with him?" said Betty.

"That's part of it," I said.

"What are you talking about?" said Betty.

"She wanted some legal advice," I said. "She got the infection in a Vietnamese restaurant in Virginia, and she wants to sue them."

"She got it from something she ate, or from the toilet seat?" said Betty.

"The toilet seat, I guess," I said, "although I'm not sure. Maybe from the spring rolls."

"Oh, God," said Betty. "Poor Thelma."

"Poor Thelma?" I said.

"I feel so sorry for her," said Betty.

"Don't feel too sorry for her," I said. "It's curable. Eventually."

"Maybe I should have her and Jonathan to dinner," said Betty.

"Don't," I said.

"Why not?" said Betty. "It's not catching, is it?"

"No," I said, "it's just that she's so depressed, she's no fun to be around."

"I think we should have a dance," said Betty.

"What?" I said.

"The three of us. You, me and Thelma."

"I hate dances," I said.

"It'll be fun, Rachel," said Betty.

"I can't dance," I said.

"Come on," said Betty. "Where do you think we should do it?"

"The White House," I said.

"That's a great idea," said Betty. "They're always talking about opening it up to the public. I'll call the social secretary."

"Betty—"

"And let's have lunch, the three of us, next week. Tuesday."

"Tuesday I have to be in New York to do a cooking demonstration."

"Rachel, you really are impossible," said Betty. "Thelma and I will have lunch on Tuesday. We will plan the dance. It will make Thelma feel better about her infection, and you'll have something to take your mind off the robbery—"

"My mind isn't *on* the robbery," I said.

"Good," said Betty. "Start making your guest list."

"Thelma's going to want to invite the

Kissingers," I said. "Is that the kind of dance you want to have?"

"Goodbye," said Betty, and hung up.

POTATOES AND LOVE: SOME REFLECTIONS

The beginning

I have friends who begin with pasta, and friends who begin with rice, but whenever I fall in love, I begin with potatoes. Sometimes meat and potatoes and sometimes fish and potatoes, but always potatoes. I have made a lot of mistakes falling in love, and regretted most of them, but never the potatoes that went with them.

Not just any potato will do when it comes to love. There are people who go on about the virtues of plain potatoes—plain boiled new potatoes with a little parsley or dill, or plain baked potatoes with crackling skins—but my own feeling is that a taste for plain potatoes coincides with cultural antecedents I do not possess, and that in any case, the time for plain potatoes—if there is ever a time for plain potatoes—is never at the beginning of something. It is also, I should add, never at the end of something. Perhaps you can get away with plain potatoes in the middle, although I have never been able to.

All right, then: I am talking about crisp potatoes. Crisp potatoes require an immense amount of labor. It's not just the peeling, which is one of the few kitchen chores no electric device has been invented to alleviate; it's also that the potatoes, once peeled, must be cut into whatever shape you intend them to be, put into water to be systematically prevented from turning a loathsome shade of bluish-brownish-black, and then meticulously dried to ensure that they crisp properly. All this takes time, and time, as any fool can tell you, is what true romance is about. In fact, one of the main reasons why you must make crisp potatoes in the beginning is that if you don't make them in the beginning, you never will. I'm sorry to be so cynical about this, but that's the truth.

There are two kinds of crisp potatoes that I prefer above all others. The first are called Swiss potatoes, and they're essentially a large potato pancake of perfect hash browns; the flipping of the pancake is so wildly dramatic that the potatoes themselves are almost beside the point. The second are called potatoes Anna; they are thin circles of potato cooked in a shallow pan in the oven and then turned onto a plate in a darling mound of crunchy brownness. Potatoes Anna is a classic French recipe, but there is something so homely and old-fashioned about them that they can usually be passed off as either an ancient family recipe or something you just made up.

For Swiss potatoes: Peel 3 large (or 4 small) russet potatoes (or all-purpose if you can't get russets) and put them in cold water to cover. Start 4 tablespoons butter and 1 tablespoon cooking oil melting in a nice heavy large frying pan. Working quickly, dry the potatoes and grate them on the grating disk of the Cuisinart. Put them into a colander and squeeze out as much water as you can. Then dry them again on paper towels. You will need more paper towels to do this than you ever thought possible. Dump the potatoes into the frying pan, patting them down with a spatula, and cook over medium heat for about 15 minutes, until the bottom of the pancake is brown. Then, while someone is watching, loosen the pancake and, with one incredibly deft motion, flip it over. Salt it generously. Cook 5 minutes more. Serves two.

For potatoes Anna: Peel 3 large (or 4 small) russet potatoes (or Idahos if you can't get russets) and put them in water. Working quickly, dry each potato and slice into $\frac{1}{16}$-inch rounds. Dry them with paper towels, round by round. Put 1 tablespoon clarified butter into a cast-iron skillet and line the skillet with overlapping potatoes. Dribble clarified butter and salt and pepper over them. Repeat twice. Put into a 425° oven for 45 minutes, pressing the potatoes down now and then. Then turn up the oven to 500° and cook 10 more minutes. Flip onto a round platter. Serves two.

The middle (I)

One day the inevitable happens. I go to the potato drawer to make potatoes and discover that the little brown buggers I bought in a large sack a few weeks earlier have gotten soft and mushy and are sprouting long and quite uninteresting vines. In addition, one of them seems to have developed an odd brown leak, and the odd brown leak appears to be the cause of a terrible odor that in only a few seconds has permeated the entire kitchen. I throw out the potatoes and look in the cupboard for a box of pasta. This is the moment when the beginning ends and the middle begins.

The middle (II)

Sometimes, when a loved one announces that he has decided to go on a low-carbohydrate, low-fat, low-salt diet (thus ruling out the possibility of potatoes, should you have been so inclined), he is signaling that the middle is ending and the end is beginning.

The end

In the end, I always want potatoes. Mashed potatoes. Nothing like mashed potatoes when you're feeling blue. Nothing like getting into bed with a bowl of hot mashed potatoes already loaded with butter, and methodically adding a thin cold slice of butter to every forkful. The problem with mashed potatoes, though, is that they require almost as much hard work as crisp potatoes, and when you're feeling blue the last thing you feel like is hard work. Of course, you can always get someone to make the mashed potatoes for you, but let's face it: the reason you're blue is that there *isn't* anyone to make them for you. As a result, most people do not have nearly enough mashed potatoes in their lives, and when they do, it's almost always at the wrong time.

(You can, of course, train children to mash potatoes, but you should know that Richard Nixon spent most of his childhood making mashed potatoes for his mother and was extremely methodical about getting the lumps out. A few lumps make mashed potatoes more authentic, if you ask me, but that's not the point. The point is that perhaps children should not be trained to mash potatoes.)

For mashed potatoes: Put 1 large (or 2 small) potatoes in a large pot of salted water and bring to a boil. Lower the heat

and simmer for at least 20 minutes, until
tender. Drain and place the potatoes back
in the pot and shake over low heat to
eliminate excess moisture. Peel. Put
through a potato ricer and immediately
add 1 tablespoon heavy cream and as
much melted butter and salt and pepper
as you feel like. Eat immediately. Serves
one.

X

I don't want to string this part out. You don't really need to hear a blow-by-blow account, because it isn't all that interesting. The first night back I made shrimp curry. (The recipe's in *Uncle Seymour's Beef Borscht* if you want it.) The next night chicken stuffed with lemons. (Marcella Hazan.) The next night, takeout from Scott's Bar-B-Q. Mark and I sat at dinner and made conversation. The word desultory applies. We talked about everything except what had happened. I tried not to cry. I tried hard not to ask where he went in the afternoon. I tried hard not to go into his office and turn it upside down looking for more evidence, but finally I decided what the hell, go take a look, how much worse can it get, and it turned out Mark had locked his office door and I couldn't get in. At one point over the weekend Mark asked me how I made my vinaigrette, but I wouldn't tell him. I figured my vinaigrette was the only thing I had that Thelma didn't (besides a pregnancy), and I could just see him learning it from me and then rushing over to her house with a jar of Grey Poupon mustard (the essential ingredient) and teaching her the wrist movement and dancing off into a sunset of arugola salads. I must seem to be putting too much emphasis on this vinaigrette of mine, but war is war.

Perhaps you are wondering whether we had sex. Normally I don't like to get into this area, because it embarrasses me, but since it's probably crossed your mind I'd better deal with it. We had sex. We always had sex. That's one of the most perplexing parts of the story; that's one of the reasons why Mark's relationship with Thelma had come as such a surprise to me. Now that I look back on it, we hadn't been doing anything particularly inventive in that department of late, but I have never been big on invention in that department. Why kid around? Every so often I browse through books full of tasteful line drawings of supplementary positions—how to do it standing and in the swimming pool and on the floor—and I'm always mystified. On the floor! Why would anyone want to do it on the floor when a bed was available? I'll tell you the truth: even sex on a beach seems to me to be going too far.

On Tuesday morning I took the shuttle to New York for my food demonstration in the Macy's housewares department. I do food demonstrations from time to time, although I do more talking than actual demonstrating. Occasionally, serious food people come to observe, and I can see them sneer as they watch my hopelessly sloppy chopping. Serious food people do not take me seriously, and they're right not to. I more or less backed into the food writing business, and before anyone in the food establishment could decide what to do with me, there I was, writing articles and doing demonstrations and appearing on television and essentially taking money from their pockets.

What they say about me is I have no real training as a cook, I'm basically a performer, I clip recipes from other people's cookbooks and pass them off as my own, I don't have an original point of view, and I am a sellout. (This last accusation always makes me cross, because I would love to be a sellout if only someone would ask.) They used to say that I was wrong about nouvelle cuisine, but I turned out to be right about it, so they don't say that anymore. My position on nouvelle cuisine is that it's silly.

What I say about them is they use too many adjectives. I hate adjectives. I also hate similes and metaphors, just can't do them, never have been able to. Anyone who wants to write about food would do well to stay away from similes and metaphors, because if you're not careful, expressions like "light as a feather" make their way into your sentences, and then where are you? The problem, though, is how to do without adjectives. If you write about food, you can't really do without them; but if you do *with* them, you run the risk of writing sentences like "The fish was juicy but the sauce was lumpy," or "The sauce was creamy but the veal was stringy," or, to sum up, "The noun was (complimentary adjective) but the other noun was (uncomplimentary adjective)." This is a particular danger for food writers who review restaurants, which I have never done and never will. You have to draw the line somewhere.

Obviously I didn't start out in life wanting to be a food writer. These days there are probably people who do—just as there are now people who start out wanting to be film critics, God help us—but I started out wanting to be a journalist. Which I became. I was a reporter for the *New York World-Telegram and Sun* and I lived in a junior two-and-a-half, and whenever I was home alone at night I cooked myself a perfect little dinner. None of your containers of yogurt for me; no, sir. I would pick a recipe from Michael Field or Julia Child and shop on the way home and spend the first part of the evening painstakingly mastering whatever dish I had chosen. Then I would sit down to eat it in front of the television set. At the time I thought this was wildly civilized behavior, but the truth is it was probably somewhat Mamie Eisenhowerish. In any case, I learned to cook. Everyone did— everyone my age, that is. This was the mid-1960s, the height of the first wave of competitive cooking. I'm always interested when people talk about the sixties in the kind of hushed tone that is meant to connote the seriousness of it all, because what I remember about the sixties was that people were constantly looking up from dessert and saying things like: "Whose mousse is this?" Once, I remember, one of my friends called up to say his marriage had ended on account of veal Orloff, and I knew exactly what he meant. It was quite mad, really. I was never completely idiotic—I never once made a quiche, for example—but I held my own, and I'm afraid that I'm still known in certain circles as the originator of a game called If You Had to Have Only One Flavor Soufflé for the Rest of Your Life, Would It Be Chocolate or Grand Marnier?

Anyway, there I was at the *World-Telegram* when the food editor retired. There was a pause before the next food editor arrived, and I was asked to fill in and write the "A Visit With" column. You know the kind of column it was: I would go to interview famous people in their homes, and they'd talk about their dinner parties and their decorators and their indispensable housekeepers, and then, in the end, they'd give me a recipe. The recipes weren't much—you'd be amazed at how many legendary hostesses tried to get away with newlywed garbage like chicken Divan and grapes with sour cream and brown sugar— but the interviews were really quite fascinating. People would say the oddest things about the servant problem and the extra-man-at-the-dinner-party problem and tipping at Christmas and how you could tell the economy was getting worse because of all the chicken you were starting to see at dinner parties. "Dark-meat chicken," one woman said to me contemptuously.

It was just a mild little column in a newspaper no one read, but as a result of it, I began to have a field of expertise. That's probably putting it too strongly—it wasn't as if I had become an expert in law or economics or seventeenth-century England—but that's how it felt: having spent my life knowing nothing much about anything (which is known as being a generalist), I suddenly knew something about something. I certainly knew enough to make jokes in the food-world language. I learned that the words "monosodium glutamate" were almost automatically funny, especially aloud, as were "The R. T. French's Mustard Tastemaker Award," "The Pillsbury Bake-Off" and "The National Chicken Cooking Contest." This gave me an edge as a food writer that almost made up for the fact that I think that certain serious food-world subjects, like coulibiac of salmon (another automatically funny phrase), are not worth bothering with.

(Another argument I have with serious food people is that they're always talking about how *creative* cooking is. "Cooking is very creative" is how they put it. Now, there's no question that there are a handful of people doing genuinely creative things with food—although a lot of it, if you ask me, seems to consist of heating up goat cheese or throwing strawberry vinegar onto calves' liver or relying excessively on the kiwi. But most cooking is based on elementary, long-standing principles, and to say that cooking is creative not only misses the point of creativity—which is that it is painful and difficult and quite unrelated to whether it is possible to come up with yet another way to cook a pork chop—but also misses the whole point of cooking, which is that it is totally mindless. What I love about cooking is that after a hard day, there is something comforting about the fact that if you melt butter and add flour and then hot stock, *it will get thick!* It's a sure thing! It's a sure thing in a world where nothing is sure; it has a mathematical certainty in a world where those of us who long for some kind of certainty are forced to settle for crossword puzzles.)

Normally I enjoy doing food demonstrations —I like giving my speech, I like the way it laces in and out of the subject of food. But when I was about halfway through the demonstration at Macy's—I was right in the middle of cooking Lillian Hellman's pot roast—I realized I was in trouble. Lillian Hellman's pot roast is the sort of recipe that makes my reputation in the food world what it is, since it contains all sorts of low-rent ingredients like a package of onion soup mix and a can of cream of mushroom soup. It even has something called Kitchen Bouquet in it, although I always leave it out. You take a nice 4-pound piece of beef, the more expensive the better, and put it into a good pot with 1 can of cream of mushroom soup, an envelope of dried onion soup, 1 large chopped onion, 3 cloves chopped garlic, 2 cups red wine and 2 cups water. Add a crushed bay leaf and 1 teaspoon each thyme and basil. Cover and bake in a 350° oven until tender, 3½ hours or so.

The reason the pot roast recipe gets to me is that it's an occasion for a point I like to make about couples in America. What I say is that I think Lillian Hellman had a remarkable effect as a literary heroine, although not the effect she was always accused of having. I have no problem with her political persona, or with her insistence on making herself the centerpiece of most of the historical conflicts of the twentieth century; but it seems to me that she invented a romantic fantasy about her involvement with Dashiell Hammett that is every bit as unrealistic as the Doris Day movies feminists prefer to blame for society's unrealistic notions about romance. The Doris Day fantasy, you may recall, is that the big man and the little woman march into the sunset together and live happily ever after. The Lillian Hellman fantasy is that the big man and the *big* woman march into the sunset together, fighting and cursing and drinking and killing turtles, but they, too, live happily ever after (until, of course, one of them dies, leaving the other free to reinvent the romance). I'm not saying that Lillian Hellman was the first writer to animate this fantasy couple—and even Hammett had a hand in it, with his Nick and Nora Charles. But Hellman's version was presented as fact, not fiction, so it makes you think it's possible. And is it?

It's a small point, just an aside that gets me through measuring the liquid ingredients, but it occurred to me as I delivered it yet another time that I had always zipped through that part of the speech as if I had somehow managed to be invulnerable to the fantasy, as if I had somehow managed to escape from or rise above it simply as a result of having figured it out. I think you often have that sense when you write—that if you can spot something in yourself and set it down on paper, you're free of it. And you're not, of course; you've just managed to set it down on paper, that's all.

The truth is that I'm at least as big a sap about romance as old Lillian was, probably even bigger.

I'll give you another example. I've written about cooking and marriage dozens of times, and I'm very smart on the subject, I'm very smart about how complicated things get when food and love become hopelessly tangled. But I realized as I stood there doing my demonstration in the middle of the Macy's housewares department that I had been as dopey about food and love as any old-fashioned Jewish mother. I loved to cook, so I cooked. And then the cooking became a way of saying I love you. And then the cooking became the easy way of saying I love you. And then the cooking became the only way of saying I love you. I was so busy perfecting the peach pie that I wasn't paying attention. I had never even been able to imagine an alternative. Every so often I would look at my women friends who were happily married and didn't cook, and I would always find myself wondering how they did it. Would anyone love me if I couldn't cook? I always thought cooking was part of the package: Step right up, it's Rachel Samstat, she's bright, she's funny, *and she can cook!*

I got so depressed and angry thinking about all this that I gave the onion an enormous whack and sent it flying into the front row of spectators, right into some lady's Literary Guild tote bag. Everyone laughed, and I tossed my head blithely as if it were the sort of thing I do all the time—which it's not—and that's when I saw Richard. Richard is my producer. (I love being able to say things like that. My producer. My doctor. My accountant. My floor man. My agent. My maid.) Richard Finkel, who produced my television show, is tall and red-haired and cannot see even with his glasses on, and he was squinting through the crowd at Macy's while I retrieved the onion. As if he weren't obvious enough already, he began to wave wildly at me, and I immediately felt better. I love Richard. That I should have spotted him at that exact moment was really quite odd: the first night Richard and I slept together, he did an imitation of his father eating an onion, and I can almost never think of raw onions without remembering him, lying naked in bed, taking mad, passionate bites of an imaginary onion and producing spectacular belches. It's a miracle I didn't fall in love with Richard on the spot, because I'm silly enough to think that any man who would imitate his father eating an onion is a suitable love object; but I didn't. I'll tell you who would have fallen in love with Richard had she been there: Brenda, my former friend and current step-relative-once-removed. Brenda was always falling in love with men whose attraction utterly mystified me, and whenever I would ask her what she saw in them, she would say things like: "He does a wonderful Sophie Tucker." Brenda fell in love with her husband Harry because he did a brilliant bit about a two-thousand-year-old man, and she always said she knew the marriage was over a week after it had begun, when she discovered that Harry had lifted the entire routine from Mel Brooks.

Richard and I slept together only a few times. We had one of those affairs that you begin by saying, "We're making a big mistake," and what you mean by that is not that you're getting in over your head but that you're just killing time. Richard and I killed a little time and then went back to being friends. Then I started seeing Mark, and Richard started seeing Helen, and things got complicated. Richard never really liked Mark, and I didn't really like Helen—that was the complication. Helen is one of those people who never say anything, not because she's shy but because she's learned—in a way I always mean to—that if you don't say anything, you make people far more nervous and self-conscious and careful around you than if you do. People like me, we just rush into the vacuum of silence people like Helen float around in; we blather and dither and yak-yakyak, and people like Helen just sit there and smile into the wind.

"Does she hate me?" I said to Richard after I first met Helen.

"Of course not," said Richard.

"Then why doesn't she ever say anything?" I asked.

"She's shy, that's all," said Richard.

"I don't think so," I said.

"You always underestimate how intimidating you are," said Richard.

"Bullshit," I said.

"He's wrong about Iran," Richard said after he first met Mark.

"Tell him," I said. "Don't talk to me about Iran. I couldn't care less."

"I tried to tell him," said Richard, "but it's very hard to interrupt a monologist."

"He's not a monologist," I said. "He just likes to talk. Some people like to talk."

"Leave Helen out of this," Richard said.

"I wasn't even thinking of Helen," I said.

"Bullshit," said Richard.

Then we all got married. It's hard when you don't like someone a friend marries. First of all, it means you pretty much have to confine your friendship to lunch, and I hate lunch. Second of all, it means that even a simple flat inquiry like "How's Helen?" is taken amiss, since your friend always thinks that what you hope he's going to say is "Dead." You feel irritated because your darling friend has married beneath himself, and he feels irritated because you don't see the virtues of his beloved. Then, if your friend's marriage fails, he becomes even more irritated at you, because if you had been a real friend, you would have prevented him physically from making the mistake, you would have locked him up in a closet until the urge to get married had passed. Of course, I tried that with Brenda, and it didn't work either. Long before we learned that Harry had pilfered the two-thousand-year-old-man routine from Mel Brooks, it was clear that he wasn't good enough for Brenda, and I made the mistake of telling her so. And when I turned out to be right, when they finally broke up after eight miserable years, was she grateful to me for tipping her off in the first place? No indeed. She slept with my husband Charlie, and as an extra bonus we all ended up with Harry's crabs.

I was dreading having to tell Richard about Mark and me; I could just imagine the look of smug satisfaction that would cross his face. But that wasn't what happened. What happened was that I finished my food demonstration and Richard swept me off to a dark bar and said, "I have to talk to you," and before I could even hold up my hand to indicate that I had to talk to him, too, he began.

"I had a vision that something horrible was wrong," said Richard. "And it is."

"A vision?" I said. It's not like Richard to talk of visions. Richard doesn't even like to hear about dreams.

"I went to have my hair cut yesterday," said Richard. "I was sitting there, trying to read the paper, and Melanie, who cuts my hair, was working away, and it suddenly crossed my mind to ask her how things were with her and Ray. She's been engaged to Ray for a couple of years. So I ask her. And she rolls her eyes. And she tells me he's fallen in love with someone else. He's come to her, he's told her he's in love with someone else, but he still wants to be friends. So she says to him, I don't want to be friends with you. And he says, why not? And she says, because you're a real shithead, that's why. Melanie looks at me and says, 'Can you believe it? Can you believe his nerve? You know what he says to me after that? He says, "You mean you're not even going to cut my hair anymore?" Can you dig this? The guy falls in love with someone else while he's engaged to me and he actually thinks I'm going to go on cutting his hair. Fuck him. What do I want with him if he wants to be such an asshole?' She rolls her eyes again, and she's snipping away, and suddenly I'm looking dead ahead into the mirror, and something weird starts to happen to me. Maybe a vision is putting it too strongly, but that's what it felt like. I thought to myself: Do not ask for whom the bell tolls, Richard Finkel, it tolls for you."

"Richard," I said, "what are you talking about?"

"I *knew*," said Richard. "At that moment I *knew*."

"You knew what?" I said.

"I knew Helen was in love with someone else."

"Helen," I said.

"My wife," said Richard. "Helen. Remember? The one you hate."

"I don't hate Helen," I said. "Helen hates me."

"It was suddenly clear," Richard said. "Helen was in love with someone else, and she was going to tell me about it, and there wasn't the remotest chance that when she did I was going to be as healthy and strong about it as this girl who cuts my hair."

"And *is* Helen in love with someone else?" I said.

"Yes," said Richard. "I came home and I told her about my vision, and when I got through, do you know what she said to me? She said, 'I think we'd better have a talk.'" Richard shook his head. "'I think we'd better have a talk' are the seven worst words in the English language."

"Helen is in love with someone else," I said.

"Yes," said Richard.

"That is really weird," I said.

"You don't know the half of it," said Richard.

"Yes I do," I said. "Ask me how Mark is."

"How's Mark?" said Richard.

"He's in love with someone else," I said.

"You're just saying that to make me feel better," said Richard.

"No I'm not," I said. "Mark has fallen in love with someone else, and he's treating me like an old beanbag."

"Oh, sweetie," said Richard, and he gave me a big hug. Then he ordered two more drinks. Doubles. Then he gave me another hug. One thing I have to say about marital crises is that people certainly do hug you a lot when you're going through them.

"Is it a boy or a girl?" said Richard.

"Is what a boy or a girl?" I said.

"The person Mark's fallen in love with," said Richard.

"I know you don't like Mark," I said, "but that is truly an absurd question."

"It's a girl, right?" said Richard.

"Right," I said.

"That's what Helen's fallen in love with, too," said Richard.

"Oh, sweetie," I said.

We looked at each other. It was a tricky moment. It's always a tricky moment when a friend tells you his marriage is in trouble: you have to be very careful what you say, in case he rides it out. This moment, however, was trickier than most. It would have been a terrible mistake, for example, for me to have said "Good riddance to bad rubbish" to Richard, although that's what I thought. It would have been an even bigger mistake for me to have introduced the word "dyke" into the conversation, but I didn't have to worry about that.

"Did you know she was a dyke?" said Richard.

"There's no way to tell if someone's a dyke,"

I said. "All sorts of attractive, feminine women are dykes. In fact, if anything, I would say that Helen isn't quite attractive enough to become one."

"That's not funny," said Richard.

"Yes it is," I said. "Anyway, she's not necessarily a dyke; she's just having a thing with a woman."

"I suppose you're going to tell me that it's normal and natural, and that all women have tendencies of that sort."

"No," I said, "but it's not as much of a stretch for women as it is for men. It's not that big a deal."

"It's a big deal if it's your wife," said Richard. "And I'll tell you the worst part of it. The worst part of it is that she's fallen in love with someone that I introduced her to. She's fallen in love with her secretary, and I got her the job."

"I'm not following you," I said.

"Joyce Raskin," said Richard. "The secretary. She used to work at Channel Thirteen, and she got laid off. I'd always liked her, and Helen was looking for a secretary, so I gave Joyce Helen's number and now she's sleeping with my wife."

"Well, don't blame Joyce," I said.

When my friend Brenda slept with my first husband, Charlie, I made that mistake—I blamed Brenda. It seemed quite unsurprising that Charlie would betray me—he, after all, was a man, and men had been betraying me

since the first grade. *But she was my friend!*
She had been my friend since the day we'd
met, when we were both five years old and
standing on line for books in kindergarten;
and I have never forgotten that moment because she turned around and I looked at her
and decided she was the most beautiful thing
I'd ever seen. Her flaxen hair came to her
waist, her eyes were deep green, her skin was
white as snow, just like a stupid fairy tale. I
always hoped that Brenda would eventually
lose her looks—my theory being that I would
grow up and gain mine, she would lose hers,
and we'd end up more or less even—but she
never did. What made this worse when we
were young was that every summer we went
to camp together and performed as an act in
the camp talent show, and she always got to
be the girl and I always had to be the boy. I
had been deeply and smolderingly resentful of
Brenda for years simply because I so wanted
to be the girl and never got to be, and the truth
is that I was secretly pleased when she slept
with Charlie because I was exonerated from
the guilt of all those years of feeling jealous of
her and was plunged suddenly into a warm
bath of innocent victimization.

That's the catch about betrayal, of course:
that it feels good, that there's something immensely pleasurable about moving from a
complicated relationship which involves
minor atrocities on both sides to a nice, neat,
simple one where one person has done some-

thing so horrible and unforgivable that the other person is immediately absolved of all the low-grade sins of sloth, envy, gluttony, avarice and I forget the other three.

It wasn't until years later, when the extent of the betrayal was finally revealed to me, that I realized how wrong I'd been to blame Brenda. Years later, Brenda, the creep, turned up at my father's wedding to her big sister and came up to me, dripping with earnest, weepy sincerity.

"I really hope we can be friends again," she said.

"I seriously doubt we're ever going to be," I said.

"But I miss you so much," said Brenda. She started to cry.

"Don't pull that on me," I said. "I didn't do anything to you, you did it to me. Remember?"

"Yes," said Brenda. "And I'll never forgive myself. Please forgive me."

Be reasonable, Rachel, I said to myself. This woman is now a relative. Are you never going to speak to her again because of one afternoon's indiscretion? Because of one afternoon your husband went out to buy light bulbs and didn't?

"Please forgive me," Brenda went on. "If I could take back any week of my life, it would be that week in Florida."

That week in Florida! I couldn't believe it! Months before the afternoon of the light bulbs, Brenda had been so forlorn about her marriage to Harry that Charlie and I had taken her along with us to the Pillsbury Bake-Off. To perk her up! Can you imagine? I had spent the week wandering through the Grand Ballroom of the Fontainebleau Hotel, judging the sweet 'n' creamy crescent crisps, and now it turned out that Brenda and Charlie had spent the week watching X-rated movies on the pay TV upstairs and fucking like rabbits. There I was at my father's wedding reception, there was my father telling yet another worn-out anecdote about how he told Howard Hawks to stuff it, there was my new step-mother passing the guacamole, and I was in such a rage about that week in Florida I could hardly see straight. I wasn't angry at Brenda, you understand. I'd spent so many years being angry at Brenda that I didn't have the energy to be any angrier. It was Charlie I wanted to kill. I'll admit it was a delayed reaction, but I honestly wanted to call him up and tell him to go to hell and threaten never to see him again. Since I really hadn't seen him since our marriage ended five years earlier, this would have been a fairly empty gesture, but I still felt like making it. I was in a real mess with Mark, no question of that, but at least I knew whom to blame.

"Why shouldn't I blame Joyce?" Richard said to me. "She was my friend."

"But Helen is your wife," I said.

"But I never trusted Helen," said Richard. "She just used to sit there and drink her Tab, and I could never figure out what was going through her head."

"Well, now you know," I said.

"What's that supposed to mean?" said Richard.

"I don't know," I said, "but it was meant to make you feel better, not to make you mad."

"I'm sorry," said Richard. "Tell me about you and Mark."

We went out to the street. It was a clear October day, and we started walking uptown, arm in arm. When you're pregnant, it's especially nice to walk arm in arm with someone who's tall, because your stomach fits in so neatly. I told him about me and Mark and Thelma. By the time I got through, we had walked all the way from Macy's to Central Park, and when we got to the park, Richard kissed me. Richard kisses very nicely. So does Mark, but one of the things that happen in marriage is that the kissing stops. We walked over to the zoo, watched the Delacorte clock strike five, and sat down on a bench facing the seal pond. Richard kissed me again.

"I think I cooked too much for him," I said.

"You're crazy," said Richard.

"I think I was so entranced with being a couple that I didn't even notice that the person I thought I was a couple with thought he was a couple with someone else."

Richard put his hand on my stomach. It was hard and round as a basketball. "I think you should come home with me," he said.

I shook my head no.

"I mean it, Rachel," said Richard. "It'll be terrific. I've never slept with anyone who was seven months pregnant."

"I'm sure Helen will like it, too," I said.

"Helen moved out this morning," said Richard. "So you can move in if you want to. There's even room for the kids. I'm serious, Rachel. I once did a documentary on Lamaze, so I'm prepared to go into labor with you. We can go take a refresher course."

"I'm not big on Lamaze," I said.

"Then we can go take a class in anti-Lamaze," said Richard.

"But we're not in love," I said.

"How do you know?" said Richard.

"Because I'm still in love with Mark. And you're still in love with Helen. And we would just huddle together, two little cuckolds in a storm, with nothing to hold us together but the urge to punish the two of them for breaking our hearts."

"Marry me," said Richard. He stood up and said it again, loudly. "Marry me, Rachel."

There were a dozen people sitting on benches and wandering around the seal pond, and I could see them turning to watch.

"I mean it, Rachel," said Richard, very loudly now. "I want to marry you. I should have married you in the first place."

"Marry him, Rachel," shouted a young man sitting two benches away. "Give the kid a father."

There was a cheer from a couple on another bench, and scattered laughs.

"Richard, sit down," I said. "Please."

"Do you want to bring a child into the world under these circumstances?" he shouted. He was moving toward the seal pond now, and he jumped onto the parapet surrounding it. "I want to marry you and you want to marry me—you just aren't in touch with it. Marry me, Rachel. I'm constant. I'm immutable. I'm probably drunk, but I mean every word of this. When I say forever, I mean forever. And if you want me to sit down and stop shouting at you and making a public spectacle of myself, you'll have to say yes." There was a huge cheer from the spectators. "You hear this?" said Richard. "There's a groundswell of support here." He looked at me and raised both hands in the air in a victory salute. "Marry me," he shouted, "and you will never have to set foot in the city of Washington again. Marry me and you will never have to pretend you know the difference between Iran and Iraq. Marry me and you will never again have to listen to someone tell you who he thinks the next assistant foreign editor of the *Washington Post* is going to be." He tossed his head and smiled in what I'm sure he thought was an extremely handsome gesture. Then he turned around and leapt backward into the seal pond. There was a huge flapping of flippers as the seals who were lying on the rocks dove into the water. Everyone ran to the fence and watched as Richard swam several circles around the pond in a perfect Australian crawl and then pulled himself up to dry on the rocks. "Think it over," he shouted to me, and then fell backward in a mock collapse. About a minute later, he was arrested by the park police for disturbing the peace. He was extremely good-humored about it. They wrapped him up in a horse blanket and took him to the precinct in the park and wrote out a ticket and sent him home. I made him some eggs and put him to bed.

"Stay here," he said.

"No," I said.

"Where are you going?"

"To my father's for the night. I've missed the last plane."

"Rachel," said Richard, "it had nothing to do with how much you cooked for him. It had nothing to do with how much you wanted to be a couple. It had nothing to do with you."

"It must have had something to do with me," I said.

"Why?" said Richard.

"Because if it didn't, there's nothing I can do about it."

"That's my point," said Richard.

"I know that's your point," I said, "but I can't accept it."

"Well, if you ever do," said Richard, "you ought to do what I did. I feel much, much better."

"Are you suggesting I ask someone I'm not

in love with to marry me and then jump into the seal pond?" I said.

"I'm suggesting that you make a wild and permanent gesture of size," said Richard, "and mine was to ask you to marry me and jump into the seal pond. Yours can be anything you want."

"The only wild and permanent gesture of size that has ever crossed my mind," I said, "is to have my hair cut."

"You'll think of something," said Richard. "And when you do, I'll be here." Then he smiled and fell asleep.

XI

*T*he next morning, I flew back to Washington. I felt better; at least someone wanted to be married to me. It wasn't the person I was married to, but it was better than nothing. I took a cab home. Maybe he's missed me, I thought as we came around the corner. Maybe he's come to his senses. Maybe he's remembered he loves me. Maybe he's full of remorse. There was a police car parked in front of the house. Maybe he's dead, I thought. That wouldn't solve everything, but it would solve a few things. He wasn't, of course. They never are. When you want them to die, they never do.

Mark was sitting in the living room with two Washington policemen. The police were telling Mark how much they liked his column and drinking beer. It's always a shock to me that the police are willing to drink your beer. I spent so many years as a child watching Jack Webb turn down beer on *Dragnet* that I've come to believe it's practically insulting to offer a policeman even a cup of coffee. When I walked in, both policemen stood up, and one of them shook my hand and announced solemnly that he had come to return my diamond ring. There was a receipt, which I signed, and then he handed me a small brown envelope tied with string. I opened it. The ring was inside, wrapped in tissue, along with a letter from Detective Nolan. "Dear Ms. Samstat," it said, "I am sending this to Washington, as I understand from your therapist that you are living there again. We caught the perpetrator and he confessed, so it will not be necessary for you to appear in court. If you turn up in New York at any point, give me a call. I am bald now." There was a phone number and his name, Andrew Nolan. Andrew. Not a bad name. Andy. AndyAndyAndy. No, Andy. Please, Andy. Yes, Andy. Don't stop, Andy. I love you, Andy. I started to put the ring back on my finger, but the diamond was loose in the setting. A sign. I was sick and tired of signs. I showed it to Mark. He glared at me. Another sign.

The police left, and Sam came rushing downstairs, shouting, "Mommy, Mommy," and jumped into my lap.

"Thelma called yesterday," Mark said, "and she's very angry at you, and I am, too."

"Where were you, Mommy?" said Sam.

"New York City," I said, "but I'm back now."

"She had lunch with Betty yesterday," said Mark, "and Betty told her you said she had herpes."

"I never said herpes," I said.

"You must have said something," said Mark.

"I said she had an infection," I said.

"Well, she's furious at you," said Mark.

"*She's* furious at *me*," I said. "That's rich." All my life I had wanted to say, "That's rich." Now I finally had gotten my chance. "That's really rich," I said. "Listen, you bastard. You tell Thelma that if she keeps calling here, I'll tell Betty she has the clap."

"Clap hands," said Sam, and clapped his together.

"I'll get it into the Ear, too," I said. " 'What hopelessly tall and ungainly Washington hostess has a social disease, and we don't mean her usual climbing?' "

Mark stood up and strode out of the room and slammed the door behind him. I heard the car start, and he drove off.

I read Sam a story, but I could barely concentrate. When is this going to stop hurting? I wondered. How was I ever going to get through? There was one bright spot in my life, my child, and I couldn't even focus on him. I've been shot in the heart, I thought. I've been shot in the brain, I thought, and all I can come up with are clichés about being shot in the heart. I knew there were women who understood these things, who could walk around as if they were under water until the smoke cleared, who could keep their big mouths shut, who could even manage the delicate moment when they confronted their rivals at a dinner or the supermarket or the Saks Jandel winter clearance sale, but I clearly wasn't one of them. My mother once caught my father kissing someone at a party, and she never forgot it; every time she got tanked she brought it up. A mere kiss. What would she have done with a full-fledged love affair during a pregnancy?

I knew it wasn't Thelma's fault that any of this had happened. She was never my friend. We had never even had lunch! And I had long since ceased to believe in the existence of that mystical sisterly loyalty women are alleged to feel toward one another. But knowing all this, I nonetheless hated her with every swollen inch of my being. I hated her for turning Mark from the man I had fallen in love with into a cold, cruel stranger; it was almost as if he had become her mirror image, and was treating me the same way Thelma treated her husband Jonathan.

I could just imagine the next Washington evening all four of us were invited to. I could just imagine Thelma doing her gracious lady number, holding out her hand like the Queen of England ready to mend a fence with an unruly colonial nation, paying me a totally hypocritical compliment about the black *schmatta* I had been stuck wearing since my fifth month of pregnancy. "Oh, Rachel," she would say, "I always find that dress so very becoming." I wanted more than anything to be a good girl under those circumstances. To button my lip. To let one go by. I wanted more than anything to be the kind of cool and confident person who could treat her as if she were no more trouble to me than an old piece of chewing gum I had accidentally stepped in. But clearly I wasn't cut out to be that kind of person.

And what would happen if everyone found out? What would happen if this tacky little mess became common knowledge; what would happen when the four of us became that year's giggle, or gossip, or simply what Walter Winchell used to call a Dontinvitem? It was hard enough putting a marriage back together without becoming known publicly as a marriage-in-trouble; a marriage-in-trouble is welcomed with about as much warmth as cancer.

I took Sam into the kitchen and handed him over to Juanita. Then I went out the back door and over to Mark's office. The door to it was open, as I'd expected; he'd left the house in such a hurry he hadn't locked it. I sat down in his desk chair and opened the drawer and pulled out the file with the phone bills in it. It was all there, as I knew it would be: local phone calls that Mark had charged to our home number; long-distance calls to France in May; calls in August to Martha's Vineyard. I pulled out the American Express bills. (What did masochistic women do before the invention of the credit card?) I went through the receipts: the Marriott Hotel in Alexandria, the Plaza Hotel in New York, the Ritz-Carlton in Boston. And the flowers—so many flowers.

I felt like a character in a trashy novel; I even knew which trashy novel I felt like a character in, which made it worse: *The Best of Everything*. At least I wasn't going through the garbage, but that was only because it hadn't turned out to be necessary. The first flowers were sent in mid-March. Mid-March. I suddenly remembered: in mid-March, when the nuclear power plant at Three Mile Island overheated, I had become so worried about its blowing contaminated air in our direction that I had taken Sam with me to a food demonstration in Atlanta. For years, Mark had been haranguing me about my total lack of interest in politics, and finally I had got interested—so interested I had actually left town—and where had it got me? It had got me and Sam to Atlanta, and my husband and Thelma to bed. That would teach me to be political.

I put the papers back into the files and shut the drawer. Then I sat there, looking out the window. There was a newspaper open on the desk. I glanced down at it and realized that I hadn't seen that day's *Post*. I stared—it *wasn't* that day's *Post*. It was the Sunday real estate section. I felt a knot in my stomach, and lost my breath for a moment. I opened it to Houses—D.C. Mark had been through the section carefully. He had marked all the houses with four bedrooms or more in decent northwest Washington locations. I closed my eyes to stop the dizziness. So they were looking at houses. Well, why was I surprised? They were looking at blazers and couches; could houses be far behind? There were little scribbled notes next to a few of the listings. Addresses. Information about maids' rooms. One of the houses appeared to have a pool.

I went back to the kitchen and sat with Sam while he had lunch. I sang "The Itsy Bitsy Spider" fourteen times. Sam went up for his nap, and I borrowed Juanita's car. I drove to Cleveland Park, where the Rices lived. I drove past their house. The shades were drawn in front; it looked as if no one was home. I was about half a block past the house, thinking about tootling over to the Marriott Hotel in Alexandria and bursting in on them with a can of Raid, when I saw our car. I stopped short and backed up. Our car, definitely. I parked and got out and stood on the curb, staring into it. There was Sam's baby seat, strapped into the back. Sam's baby seat was always strapped into the back of the car, but somehow, at this moment, it seemed the ultimate obscenity—Mark's involving even the baby seat in his affair.

I walked up to the house and looked for signs of life. The Rices lived in a large wood house bordered by rhododendron and azalea bushes. I stepped onto the lawn and tried to see through a crack below a drawn window shade, but the bushes were in the way. I was trying to move quietly, but there were crunching leaves and twigs everywhere I stepped. Suddenly I tripped and fell. I realized I'd twisted my ankle, and for a moment I thought I'd strained my stomach muscles, but the pain went away. I looked to see what I'd tripped on and saw that it was a wire that surrounded the house. I began to follow it to see where it led, turned the corner, and gasped. There was a body lying face down on the ground under a rhododendron bush. Jonathan Rice. Maybe he's dead, I thought. It crossed my mind as his leg twitched that I had had that thought twice in less than two hours about two completely different men, and I couldn't decide which of them I was more disappointed to find out I was wrong about.

Jonathan was lying there wearing a set of earphones. He turned and looked at me. He barely blinked. He took off the earphones and sat up.

"You really shouldn't have said that thing about the herpes, you know," he said. "Thelma was very fond of you."

"But now she's not," I said.

"Now she's not," said Jonathan. "Now she's very angry. And they're looking at houses. And they found something they like on Twenty-first Street, but Thelma thinks they need five bedrooms and Mark thinks they can make do with four."

I wondered who was handling the Middle East while Jonathan was out spying in the bushes, but he had put on the earphones again, and now he was shaking his head. "They're talking about buying it right away and getting it all ready, and a few months after you have the baby Mark and Thelma will move in. He thinks he can get joint custody."

I was having trouble breathing again, and I put my hand on my stomach.

"What's the matter?" said Jonathan.

"I tripped on your wire," I said, "and I think I strained my stomach muscles."

A few minutes later, as Jonathan was giving me the next bulletin—something about how Mark and Thelma were going to finance the purchase with a bank loan, which Jonathan took as an occasion to lecture me on rising interest rates—I had another pain.

"Jonathan," I said.

Jonathan put his fingers to his lips, as if something really cosmic were going on in the house.

I pulled the earphones from his head.

"Jonathan," I said. "I'm in labor."

* * *

I don't remember very much. I remember that Jonathan sprang to his feet and bounded into the house. I remember that Mark came out a few minutes later. I remember the drive to the hospital: I accused Mark of looking at houses; he accused me of snooping in places I didn't belong. I remember the labor room, and my obstetrician suddenly appearing, Marvin, my obstetrician, taking charge, being a professor, explaining my labor to a group of interns: the baby is in the transverse position and we can't risk waiting for it to turn itself, given the prematurity; another Caesarean is indicated. Are there any questions? One of the interns raised his hand. "I really enjoy your column," he said to Mark. The interns left. "Your husband can watch," Marvin said to me. "It really isn't allowed with Caesareans, but we'll sneak him into the delivery room." He was so pleased with himself, Marvin was, so pleased that he would be able to give this lovely couple he was on a first-name basis with the opportunity to share in the birth of their second child. Wrong couple, I wanted to say; that was last year's couple. This year things are different. This year my husband is a stranger. Do not let this stranger see me eviscerated.

The anesthetist put the needle into my back and I waited for the epidural to grab hold. Mark was standing next to me. One contraction. Two contractions. Three. Then the dullness, the easing off, the mermaid sensation. I watched the fetal monitor bleeping steadily as they wheeled me into the delivery room.

"Tell me about when Sam was born," I said to Mark.

He looked at me.

"Start where the doctor says there's something wrong," I said.

Mark nodded. "The doctor took me outside the labor room and said there was something wrong, they were losing the heartbeat. And we went back in and he told you the baby was in distress. And you said, 'Is our baby going to die?'"

I had heard this dozens of times.

Mark went on: "And he said, 'We're going to do an emergency Caesarean.' And they took you away. You were really brave. I was terrified. And I sat out in the waiting room, and the man sitting across from me was eating a sausage pizza. And fifteen minutes later the doctor came out, and took me into the delivery room, and there was Sam, making these funny little noises. They put him into my arms, and you woke up and you said, 'Is that our baby?' And I laid him down on you. And I lay down next to you."

I was crying.

"That was a great day," I said.

"Can you feel this?" said the doctor. The knife.

"Yes," I said. "A little."

I turned my head away from Mark. A nurse

wiped my face and said, hold on, it's going to be all right. The pediatrician, our pediatrician, came into the delivery room. "If I am going to be your pediatrician," he had said when Sam was born, "we are going to have to understand something. You are never to call me and say, 'I'm sorry to bother you.' You are never to call me and say, 'This is probably nothing.' If you think it's worth a phone call, I want to hear about it. Got it?" Mark and I had sat there with our floppy little bundle. We were so proud—so proud of ourselves, of our baby, even of our pediatrician's patter. We marched into parenthood so full of hubris. We were on our second marriages; we had got the kinks out of the machinery; we would bring up our children in a poppy field of love and financial solvency and adequate household help. There would be guns for our daughters and dolls for our sons.

After Sam was born, I remember thinking that no one had ever told me how much I would love my child; now, of course, I realized something else no one tells you: that a child is a grenade. When you have a baby, you set off an explosion in your marriage, and when the dust settles, your marriage is different from what it was. Not better, necessarily; not worse, necessarily; but different. All those idiotically lyrical articles about sharing child-rearing duties never mention that, nor do they allude to something else that happens when a baby is born, which is that all the power struggles of the marriage have a new playing field. The baby wakes up in the middle of the night, and instead of jumping out of bed, you lie there thinking: Whose turn is it? If it's your turn, you have to get up; if it's his turn, then why is he still lying there asleep while you're awake wondering whose turn it is? Now it takes *two* parents to feed the child—one to do it and one to keep the one who does it company. Now it takes two parents to take the child to the doctor—one to do it and one to keep the one who does it from becoming resentful about having to do it. Now it takes two parents to fight over who gets to be the first person to introduce solids or the last person to notice the diaper has to be changed or the one who cares most about limiting sugar snacks or the one who cares least about conventional discipline.

No one ever tells you these things—not that we would have listened had anyone tried. We were so smart. We were so old. We were so happy. We had it knocked.

"Can you feel this?" the doctor said.

"No."

He was cutting now. Far, far away. A minute passed. Then two. Let the baby be okay, please let him be okay. I opened my eyes and saw a nurse crossing the room to the pediatrician. In her arms I could see the baby's wet head and spiky black hair. I could see an arm,

such a skinny arm. Long skinny legs. *Move.
Please move.* A flutter kick. A noise like a tiny
cough. A tiny cry.

Nathaniel.

I closed my eyes.

He was fine, I could hear them saying that.
He's fine. He's going to be fine.

So. Nathaniel was early. I could hardly
blame him. Something was dying inside me,
and he had to get out.

XII

It was a complicated Caesarean, and there were complications. Nathaniel was on the eighth floor of the hospital, with tubes and monitors stuck all over his little froggy body, and I was on the fifth, with tubes and monitors all over mine. I lay in bed in a Percodan haze; I spent hours turning my marriage over in my mind. What had happened? What had gone wrong? *He was crazy.* I kept coming back to that. It was a simple enough answer, but accepting that answer meant accepting that I would never really know what had happened, accepting the mystery. I hate mystery, and I'm not the only one who does. Nature abhors a mystery too.

Vera flew to Washington. She spent a day with me in the hospital. She rubbed my head and listened while I floated trial balloons at her. I told her I thought I had spent too much time cooking and not enough time paying attention. I told her I thought that having a baby had changed our lives together. I told her I had been impatient and mean and snappish and irritable, and that it was no wonder Mark was drawn to someone who hadn't heard all his stories before and didn't shoot him a reproving look every time he uttered an opinion he had stolen from his best friend.

"All this may be true," Vera said, "but it isn't the point. The point is to figure out what you want."

"Maybe we just ran out of things to renovate," I said. "Maybe that was the problem. Maybe if we'd just gone on buying houses and fighting with contractors and arguing over whether to bleach the floor or stain it dark, we would have lived happily ever after."

"Did you hear me?" Vera said.

"I actually believed it was possible to have a good marriage," I said.

"It is possible," said Vera.

"No it's not," I said. "And don't tell me about your marriage, I don't want to hear about it. You got the last good one. For the rest of us, it's hopeless. I know that, but I never really get it. I go right on. I think to myself: I was wrong about the last one, but I'll try harder to be right about the next one."

"That's not the worst lesson to take through life," said Vera.

"But it doesn't work," I said. "It's kreplach. Remember?"

Vera looked at me, and her eyes filled with tears. She does this sometimes, especially when I'm being hateful and difficult; she responds by having all the feelings I'm refusing to have. Now she reached over and took my hand, and we both began to cry.

Mark came to the hospital every day. Every day except for Thelma's birthday. On Thelma's birthday, he called to say he had to go to New York for an interview. I know it was Thelma's birthday because Betty called the next day to tell me all about it. It seems that Jonathan Rice had planned a surprise birthday lunch for Thelma, and everyone gathered in the restaurant, ready to pop out from under the table when she arrived, but she never turned up.

"Can you imagine?" said Betty.

"I'm afraid I can," I said.

"I wish I could figure out who she's sleeping with," Betty said.

"It's probably Mark," I said.

Betty laughed. "Rachel, wait till I tell that to Mark," she said. "It'll kill him."

"I'll tell him myself," I said. "He just turned up."

"What was that about?" Mark said.

Stifle yourself, Rachel.

"Nothing," I said. "Just the Ladies' Central."

I got out of bed and into a wheelchair. Mark wheeled me and my intravenous equipment to the elevator and we went up to see the baby. We were lucky. I kept telling myself that. Nathaniel was on a floor with newborns who had real problems—there were blue babies, babies missing kidneys, babies with holes in their hearts—and there was nothing wrong with him except that he was small. He wasn't even the smallest. Still, he was ours, and he looked like a sack of bones. They'd shaved his head for the monitors, and there were tiny Band-Aids all over his body, taping the tubes here and there. We couldn't hold him. All we could do was reach in through the holes with our hexachlorophene-scrubbed hands and feed him, awkwardly propping up his floppy body by the neck. He had weighed four pounds when he was born. He was feeding well, catching up, but he was such a tiny thing. I waved a little red clown we'd put into the Isolette in front of his face. Maybe he saw it. Mark sang him a song. *Hush-a-bye, don't you cry, go to sleep-y, little baby*. I wondered where they had gone to celebrate her birthday. *When you wake you shall have all the pretty little horses*. I wondered what he had given her for her birthday. *Blacks and bays, dapples and grays, all the pretty little horses*. I wish I'd known it was Thelma's birthday; I would have sent her a present myself. *Hush-a-bye, don't you cry, go to sleep-y, little baby*. A garrote.

Arthur and Julie came to see me. One day while I was in the hospital, they discovered that their decorator had taken the four thousand dollars they had given him for furniture and spent it all on cocaine. The next day, their daughter was suspended from school for flushing six gerbils down the lavatory toilet. The next day, a bat moved into their kitchen. They brought me all of it, every day, and Julie rustled up a hairdresser to come wash my hair, and Arthur made rice pudding the day they took the tube out of my nose and I could eat bland food. Rice pudding is the only thing Arthur cooks, but he cooks it perfectly, with exactly the right proportion of rice to raisins. There's an awful lot of nursery food in this book already, so I won't give you the recipe. My feeling about rice pudding is that if you like it, you already have a good recipe; and if you don't, there's no way anyone will ever get you to eat it, unless you fall in love with someone who likes rice pudding, which I once did, and then you learn to love it, too.

My last day in the hospital, Marvin, my obstetrician, took out the stitches. Then he swiped an apple from a big basket of fruit Betty's boyfriend had sent me, and he sat down in a leatherette chair. I suspected he was going to ask if I was having a postpartum depression, but the last thing I wanted was for my obstetrician to know that in my case a postpartum depression would be superfluous. I am very fond of Marvin, even though he once asked me to endorse his book on premenstrual tension, but I wasn't up for a heart-to-heart talk with him.

"Do you believe in love?" said my obstetrician.

This is what I get for calling him by his first name, I thought. This is the price I pay for insisting that if he's going to call me by my first name I get to call him by his. Do I ask him if he gets turned on sticking his hands into ladies' pussies? Do I ask him if he gets off feeling their breasts for lumps?

"What?" I said.

"Do you believe in love?" he said.

Sometimes I believe that love dies but hope springs eternal. Sometimes I believe that hope dies but love springs eternal. Sometimes I believe that sex plus guilt equals love, and sometimes I believe that sex plus guilt equals good sex. Sometimes I believe that love is as natural as the tides, and sometimes I believe that love is an act of will. Sometimes I believe that some people are better at love than others, and sometimes I believe that everyone is faking it. Sometimes I believe that love is essential, and sometimes I believe that the only reason love is essential is that otherwise you spend all your time looking for it.

"Yes," I said. "I do."

I went home.

Nathaniel stayed in the hospital.

Both of us got stronger.

I behaved myself.

I said very little.

I attempted to follow the budget debate.

I went to a dinner party and held up my end.

They took Nathaniel out of the Isolette and I could hold him and feed him.

I read Sam a lot of stories about baby brothers.

I did not say, how are you, how are we, do you still love her, do you love me at all, are you still thinking of buying a house with her, what did you get her for her birthday, is it over with her, is it ever going to be over.

Two weeks passed.

Betty called. She asked if we wanted to come to dinner. "We have lobsters," she said. "You bring dessert. Bring one of your Key lime pies."

XIII

*I*f I had it to do over again, I would have made a different kind of pie. The pie I threw at Mark made a terrific mess, but a blueberry pie would have been even better, since it would have permanently ruined his new blazer, the one he bought with Thelma. But Betty said bring a Key lime pie, so I did. The Key lime pie is very simple to make. First you line a 9-inch pie plate with a graham cracker crust. Then beat 6 egg yolks. Add 1 cup lime juice (even bottled lime juice will do), two 14-ounce cans sweetened condensed milk, and 1 tablespoon grated lime rind. Pour into the pie shell and freeze. Remove from freezer and spread with whipped cream. Let sit five minutes before serving.

I realize now that I should have thrown the pie (or at least done the thinking that led to the throwing of the pie) several weeks earlier than I did, but it's very hard to throw a pie at someone when you're pregnant, because you feel so vulnerable. Also, let's face it, I wasn't ready to throw the pie. I should add that the pie was hardly the first thing I'd thought of throwing at Mark, but every other time I'd wanted to throw something at him, I couldn't bring myself to do it. Once, for example, right after I found out about him and Thelma, I'd been seized by a violent impulse, but the only thing I could see to throw at the time was a signed Thonet chair, and I am far too bourgeois to throw a signed Thonet anything at anyone. Some time later, especially while I was in the hospital, I gave considerable thought to smashing Mark's head in with a very good frying pan I had bought at the Bridge kitchenware company, but I always knew I would never do anything of the sort, and in any case, smashing your husband's head in with a frying pan seems slightly too fraught with feminist content, if you know what I mean.

(Even now, I wonder if I would have thrown the pie had we been eating in Betty's dining room. Probably not. On the floor in Betty's dining room is a beautiful Oriental rug, and I would have been far too concerned about staining it. Fortunately, though, we were eating in the kitchen, and the kitchen has a linoleum floor. That's how bourgeois I am: at the split second I picked up the pie to throw it at Mark, at the split second I was about to do the bravest—albeit the most derivative—thing I had ever done in my life, I thought to myself: Thank God the floor is linoleum and can be wiped up.)

On Saturday afternoon, after Betty called, I went out for a walk to buy the pie ingredients. I took Sam with me. We had a long talk about how Nathaniel would be coming home from the hospital on Monday, and how much Sam was going to love him, and how he was going to feed him some delicious spiders. We bought the food at Neam's. It was a beautiful day, so we decided to walk down to the toy store on M Street. On the way we passed the jewelry store where Mark had bought me the diamond ring, and I remembered that I hadn't yet taken it in to have it fixed. It was in a little envelope in my purse.

I could see Leo Rothman, the owner, sitting on a stool behind the counter—Leo, the dear, white-haired man who had marched with the Abraham Lincoln Brigade in the thirties and been thrown out of the Labor Department in the forties and was now a millionaire jeweler who buzzed only white people through his electronically operated door. He buzzed me in and gave me a big kiss. When Mark was courting me, when he was pursuing me with flowers and balloons and jewels, Leo was the man Mark bought the jewels from, and as a result Leo felt almost proprietary about our marriage: he had outfitted the courtship, the

wedding, the birth of the first child, the first
child's silver spoon; and he didn't seem to
mind that except for the diamond ring, none
of Mark's purchases had amounted to more
than a few hundred dollars.

I told Leo about the robbery, and he said it
would take just a minute to reset the stone.
Sam and I waited while he got out his instru-
ments and went to work. We were making
conversation. Chitchat. Nothing much. He
said did I know the diamond in the ring was a
perfect stone. I said Mark had told me that.
He said it wasn't the kind of diamond I'd ever
have trouble selling if I ever wanted to—he
had told Mark he'd be glad to buy it back for
what Mark had paid for it. I said I was glad to
hear that. He asked me how I liked the necklace. The necklace, I said. Leo looked up, and
the loup dropped from his eye. "I must be
thinking of another customer," he said.

"No you're not," I said. "I knew Mark had
bought something while I was in the hospital." So he had bought her a necklace for her
birthday. I was lying in the hospital with a
tube up my nose and he had bought her a
necklace. "That rascal," I said.

"I shouldn't have said anything," Leo said.

"I'm glad you did," I said. "Now I know
what to be prepared for. There's nothing
worse than opening a box with a necklace in it
when you're not in the mood for a necklace." I
kept talking, I couldn't stop. "Once," I said, "I
was in the mood for a nightgown, and Mark

kept dropping hints about what he'd gotten me for my birthday, and finally I said, 'I don't care what it is as long as it's not a suitcase,' and it was a suitcase. Was my face red." Leo was focused on the ring again; I'd bored him so thoroughly he barely grunted a response. He finished resetting the stone and handed the ring back to me. It was such a beautiful ring. The diamond caught the afternoon sun and made a rainbow on the wall of the store. Sam ran to the reflection, and I waved the ring this way and that, moving the rainbow while he giggled and leapt and tried to catch it in his hands.

"How much?" I said.

"No charge," Leo said.

"How much for the ring?" I said. "How much would you give me for the ring?"

Leo looked at me.

"You don't really want to sell it," he said.

"I really want to sell it," I said. "Do you really want to buy it?"

"Of course," he said.

"I love the ring, Leo," I said, "but it really doesn't go with my life. It would never have been stolen in the first place if I hadn't been wearing it on the subway, and if you've got a ring you can't wear on the subway, what's the point of having it? It's sort of like a mink coat. If I had a mink coat, I'd have to take cabs every time I was in New York, and the next thing you know we'd be even broker than we are now. Mark's so romantic, he probably spent every penny of his savings on the necklace."

Leo nodded. "For the down payment," he said.

"For the down payment," I said.

"It's a beautiful necklace," said Leo.

"Now I'll have a necklace I won't be able to wear on the subway either," I said. "How much for the ring?"

"Fifteen thousand," Leo said.

"Fifteen thousand," I said.

"That's what Mark paid for it," Leo said.

Right after my mother left my father and ran off to New Mexico with Mel, my father gave me some money. It was quite unexpected. I had gone over to visit him—I was married to Charlie at the time—and in the middle of a long and rather sentimental conversation about how termites had once eaten the entire garage door of our house in Beverly Hills one Sunday when we weren't looking, my father whipped out his checkbook and wrote me a check for three thousand dollars. "But why?" I said, hoping he wouldn't notice I had snatched it from his hands and stuffed it into my back pocket. "Because you're a good girl," said my father. I put my hand over the pocket, as if the check were going to fly right out and back into the checkbook and erase itself. I could feel the paper through the cloth; I kept running my finger over the outside of the pocket and feeling the check crinkle inside. My heart started to pound: I realized I had just been given the means to walk out of my marriage.

"Fifteen thousand it is," I said to Leo. Ten years had passed; the cost of walking out of a marriage had gone up.

I went home with Leo's check and made the pie. I was in a trance. Well, perhaps it wasn't a trance, but it was as close to a trance as I'll ever get: I was speechless. I said nothing—nothing at all—for several hours. At eight, Mark and I took the pie to Betty's. It was just us—me, Mark, Betty and Dmitri, whom Betty lives with. Dmitri used to be the Yugoslavian ambassador to the United States. When his tour ended, he went back to Belgrade and opened a chain of laundromats. Then he moved back to Washington and went into high-priced sherbet. Mark always used to throw Dmitri in my face as an example of someone who managed to be interested in food and politics simultaneously, but the truth is that what Dmitri was really interested in was money; to the extent that he was at all political, it lay in his understanding that in a socialist country you can get rich by providing necessities, while in a capitalist country you can get rich by providing luxuries. Dmitri is the most good-natured man I have ever known, which infuriates Betty, which makes Dmitri laugh, which makes Betty laugh. They seem very happy together. Not that you can tell. Look at all the people who thought Mark and I were happy. Me included.

When we got to Betty's, Mark and Dmitri went into the kitchen to boil the lobsters, and Betty and I sat in the living room while Betty talked about the dance she and Thelma and I were apparently giving. Apparently we were giving it at the Sulgrave Club. Apparently the crepe man had already been booked. Apparently all that was lacking was my guest list: Thelma and Betty had already drawn up theirs. Apparently the Kissingers were on Thelma's list, just as I'd predicted. I sat and listened and drank an entire bottle of white wine as Betty went on and on, and by the time I got to dinner, I was tipsy. We ate the lobsters. I don't remember the conversation. I do remember realizing that no one seemed to be noticing that I hadn't said anything the entire evening, and that no one seemed to mind. I must try this again, I thought; I must try again someday to sit still and not say a word. Maybe when I'm dead.

After the lobsters, I took the Key lime pie out of the freezer and put the whipped cream on it and sat it in front of me. I was going to give it five minutes to thaw slightly (see recipe). And that's when Betty turned to me and said, "Rachel, you didn't tell me about Richard and Helen!"

"What about Richard and Helen?" said Mark.

"They're getting a divorce," said Betty. "I bumped into him this week in New York."

"I always hated that woman," said Mark.

"I sort of liked her," said Dmitri.

"When did you meet her?" said Betty.

"Here," said Dmitri. "Rachel and Mark brought them over one night. No one else would talk to her, so I did. She wasn't so bad."

"You're the only person on this earth who's ever found anything even halfway nice to say about her," said Betty.

"I did think she was a dyke," said Dmitri.

"That makes me so furious!" Betty screamed. "Why didn't you tell me?"

"I did tell you," said Dmitri, "and you said, 'Don't be ridiculous.'"

"Goddammit," said Betty.

"Why are you angry at Dmitri?" said Mark.

"Because she *is* a dyke," said Betty.

"No shit," said Mark.

"And if Dmitri wasn't so good-natured about everything, he would have put it more forcefully, and I might have believed him, and then none of this would have come as a surprise to me." She glared at Dmitri. "I hate surprises," she said.

Dmitri stood up to go make the coffee and on his way he kissed Betty on the neck. "Don't try to make up to me," said Betty. She was smiling.

"Helen's a dyke?" said Mark.

"She left Richard for her secretary," said Betty.

"Did you know this, Rachel?" said Mark.

I nodded.

"I couldn't get over it," said Betty. "I kept

thinking about it on the shuttle on the way home. How could you know someone for that long . . . how long have they been together?"

"As long as Rachel and I have," said Mark.

"Exactly," said Betty. "How could you be with someone that long, be *married* to them, and not know?"

"He has to have known," said Dmitri. "*I* knew."

"He says he didn't know," said Betty. "But how could he not? How could you be married to someone and not know something like that?"

"Maybe it wasn't true when he first met her," said Dmitri.

"Of course it was true," said Betty. "You don't just become a dyke, bang, like that."

"Sure you do," said Dmitri. "It's like being allergic to strawberries. You eat strawberries all your life and then one day, bang, you get hives."

"Don't be ridiculous," said Betty.

"The last time you said 'Don't be ridiculous' to me, I was trying to tell you that Richard's wife was a dyke," said Dmitri.

"And now you're trying to tell me she was merely an incipient dyke," said Betty. "Which is it?"

"I have no idea," said Dmitri. "I'm just trying to drive you crazy." He kissed her again.

"I don't believe people change that much," said Betty. "And don't tell me they do, Rachel.

Don't give me that New York psychological bullshit about how people are capable of it. They aren't. Which brings me back to my question: how is it possible to be married to someone and not know something so fundamental?"

I was starting to get dizzy.

Perhaps I ought to say something, I thought. Either that or I'm going to fall into the pie. Perhaps I ought to say that it *is* possible. I could hear Mark changing the subject. He was saying something about Zbigniew Brzezinski. Perhaps I ought to say that you can love someone—or want to love someone—so much that you don't see anything at all. You decide to love him, you decide to trust him, you're in the marriage, in the day-to-dayness of the marriage, and you kind of notice that things aren't what they were, but it's a distant bell, it's through a filter. And then when something does turn out to be wrong, it isn't that you knew all along, it's that you were somewhere else.

"He must have been living in a dream," said Betty. She stood up to get the coffee cups. Mark and Dmitri were discussing détente.

In a dream. I suppose so. And then the dream breaks into a million tiny pieces. The dream dies. Which leaves you with a choice: you can settle for reality, or you can go off, like a fool, and dream another dream.

I looked across the table at Mark. I still love you, I thought. I still look at that dopey face of yours, with that silly striped beard, and think you are the handsomest man I've ever known. I still find you interesting, even if right now you are being more boring than the Martin Agronsky show. But someday I won't anymore. And in the meantime, I'm getting out. I am no beauty, and I'm getting on in years, and I have just about enough money to last me sixty days, and I am terrified of being alone, and I can't bear the idea of divorce, but I would rather die than sit here and pretend it's okay, I would rather die than sit here figuring out how to get you to love me again, I would rather die than spend five more minutes going through your drawers and wondering where you are and anticipating the next betrayal and worrying about whether my poor, beat-up, middle-aged body with its Caesarean scars will ever turn you on again. I can't stand feeling sorry for myself. I can't stand feeling like a victim. I can't stand hoping against hope. I can't stand sitting here with all this rage turning to hurt and then to tears. I CAN'T STAND NOT TALKING!

I looked at the pie sitting right there in front of me and suddenly it began to throb. They were talking about the State Department now. If I throw this pie at him, I thought to myself, he will never love me. And then it hit me: he *doesn't* love me. It hit me with a shimmering clarity: that was all there was to it. It didn't matter if he was crazy. It didn't matter if I was innocent or guilty. Nothing mattered except that he didn't love me. *If I throw this pie at him, he will never love me. But he doesn't love me anyway. So I can throw the pie if I want to.* I picked up the pie, thanked God for the linoleum floor, and threw it. It landed mostly on the right side of Mark's face, but that was good enough. The cream and the lime filling clung to his beard and his nose and his eyelashes, and pieces of crust dropped onto his blazer. I started to laugh. Mark started to laugh, too; I must say he handled it very well. He laughed as if all this were part of a running joke we'd forgotten to let Betty and Dmitri in on. He wiped himself off. He said, "I think it's time for us to go home." He stood up. So did I. I turned to Betty, who was staring wide-eyed at the two of us. "By the way," I said, "I'm not coming to the dance." And we went home.

Of course I'm writing this later, much much later, and it worries me that I've done what I usually do—hidden the anger, covered the pain, pretended it wasn't there for the sake of the story. "Why do you feel you have to turn everything into a story?" Vera once asked me. I remember when she asked me, in fact. It was right after my marriage to Charlie broke up, and I was living in an apartment where everything made into something else—the couch made into a bed, the coffee table made into a dining table, the end table made into a stool. "How are you?" people would ask me, in that intimate way people asked the question in those days. How *are* you. I couldn't bear it. So I told them about my apartment where everything made into something else. Then a friend called and said, "I have one piece of advice for you. I give it to all my friends whose marriages break up: Don't buy anything at Azuma." I added that to my repertoire.

Vera said: "Why do you feel you have to turn everything into a story?"

So I told her why:

Because if I tell the story, I control the version.

Because if I tell the story, I can make you laugh, and I would rather have you laugh at me than feel sorry for me.

Because if I tell the story, it doesn't hurt as much.

Because if I tell the story, I can get on with it.

My last day in Washington I read the Sunday papers. I made French toast for Sam. I went to the hospital to see Nathaniel. I asked the pediatrician if Nathaniel could go to New York when he got out of the hospital the next day. The pediatrician said he could if he took the train. I called Nathaniel's baby nurse and told her we would be going to New York on the train the next day. I called Richard in New York and told him we would be moving in for a

few weeks, until I found an apartment. I
came home and started dinner. I made a
bouillabaisse, and crème brulée, and in between there was a salad. I taught Mark to
make the vinaigrette. Mix 2 tablespoons Grey
Poupon mustard with 2 tablespoons good red
wine vinegar. Then, whisking constantly
with a fork, slowly add 6 tablespoons olive oil,
until the vinaigrette is thick and creamy; this
makes a very strong vinaigrette that's perfect
for salad greens like arugola and watercress
and endive.

We got into bed and Mark put his arms
around me. "That was a lovely evening," he
said. He fell asleep. I lay there. Two years
earlier, when I had been pregnant with Sam,
Mark would sing me a song every night and
every morning. We called it the Petunia song.
It was a dumb song, really dumb. Mark would
make up a different tune and lyrics each time,
but it never rhymed, and it was never remotely melodious. *I sing to you, Petunia, I sing a
song of love, I sing to you even though you
are bigger than the last time I sang the
Petunia song to you.* Something like that. Or:
*Oh, Petunia, I sing to thee, even though it's
much too early and I have a hangover.* You
get the idea. Really dumb, but every time
Mark sang it, I felt secure and loved in a way I
had never dreamed possible. I had always
meant to write down some of the words, because they were so silly and funny and made

me feel so happy; but I never did. And now I couldn't remember them. I could remember the feeling, but I couldn't really remember the words.

Which was not the worst way to begin to forget.

RECIPE INDEX